Nailed

ALSO BY OPAL CAREW

Nailed

Opal Carew

ST. MARTIN'S GRIFFIN

NEW YORK

This is a work of fiction. All of the characters, organizations, and events portrayed in this novel are either products of the author's imagination or are used fictitiously.

NAILED. Copyright © 2016 by Elizabeth Batten-Carew. All rights reserved. Printed in the United States of America. For information, address St. Martin's Press, 175 Fifth Avenue, New York, N.Y. 10010.

www.stmartins.com

Library of Congress Cataloging-in-Publication Data

Names: Carew, Opal, author.
Title: Nailed / Opal Carew.
Description: First edition. | New York : St. Martin's Griffin, 2016.
Identifiers: LCCN 2016012741| ISBN 9781250052872 (trade paperback) |
    ISBN 9781466854734 (e-book)
Subjects: | BISAC: FICTION / Romance / Adult. | FICTION /
    Romance / Contemporary. | GSAFD: Love stories. | Erotic fiction.
Classification: LCC PR9199.4.C367 N35 2016 | DDC 813/.6—dc23
LC record available at https://lccn.loc.gov/2016012741

Our books may be purchased in bulk for promotional, educational, or business use. Please contact your local bookseller or the Macmillan Corporate and Premium Sales Department at 1-800-221-7945, extension 5442, or by e-mail at MacmillanSpecialMarkets@macmillan.com.

First Edition: August 2016

10 9 8 7 6 5 4 3 2

To Mark,
who puts up with my nail polish obsession
with love and a big smile.
Love you!

Acknowledgments

Thank you to Rose, my wonderful editor, for indulging me in my passion on this one. Thanks to Emily, my fabulous agent, who is always there for me.

As always, thanks to Mark, Matt, and Jason for your love and encouragement.

A special thank-you to the wonderful Amy Milder of Literary Lacquers for bringing my vision of the nail polish collection in this book to life.

You can learn more about Amy and her lovely nail polishes at: www.etsy.com/shop/LiteraryLacquer.

For details about the nail polish collection, check Amy's shop or go to www.OpalCarew.com/Nailed.

Nailed

Chapter One

"Oh my God, I can't believe someone is willing to pay five thousand dollars to have dinner with me." River stared at the Kickstarter page on her cell.

"Really?" her friend Tia said. "Let me see."

Tia pushed her long, red hair behind her ear as she peered over River's shoulder. They were standing in the break room of Giselle's, the cosmetics and accessories store where they worked. River was just checking her e-mails before she stashed her phone and other belongings in her locker and started her shift.

"Hey, your campaign looks like it's fully funded," Tia observed. "That was fast. Didn't you just start it up?"

River nodded. "Two days ago." She was shocked as she stared at the numbers. Tia was right.

"So have you figured out where you're going to take this person? It better be a pretty nice place if they're paying that much."

River's stomach clenched as she shook her head, opening the next e-mail. She'd never thought anyone would actually pay that much. She knew most campaigns had some extravagant options people could buy in order to get online donors to contribute to a business initiative. She'd thought of having the person's initial tattooed on her thigh, but then discovered that someone else had done something similar. Then Tia suggested the dinner thing.

River had her own nail polish blog and had built up a bit of a following, but she never thought anyone would be enough of a fangirl to pay that much to meet her. In fact, the thought made her a bit nervous.

"Look," Tia said, still reading the next e-mail over her shoulder. "She wants to do it on Saturday. And she's even picked the place." Tia glanced at River. "Can you afford dinner at the Carousel?"

"When she's paying five grand I can."

River turned off her phone and pushed her purse into the locker next to Tia's then closed the door.

"Hello there. River, isn't it?"

River glanced up from straightening the display of lipsticks and nail polishes into the face of the handsome customer. She recognized him from yesterday when he'd come in with his wife or girlfriend. He'd bought a lot of items for her, mostly high-end nail polishes and a few pieces of the boutique's designer costume jewelry.

"Yes, sir." River smiled. "Are you back for that onyx necklace for your friend?"

He smiled, his gaze gliding over her in a way that made her uncomfortable. "No, actually. I was hoping that maybe you'd join me for a drink when you finish work."

Good God, he had to be kidding. She knew he had a girlfriend. *He knew she knew* he had a girlfriend.

"I'm sorry, sir, but I'm seeing someone."

He shrugged. "So?"

Her skin quivered in revulsion.

"I spent a lot of money here. I assume you made quite a bit in commission."

Anger surged to the surface and the polite comeback she'd fought to utter slipped away. "Does that approach actually ever get you anywhere? Because—"

But suddenly Tia grabbed her arm, startling her. "River, time for your break. I'll take over here."

Tia hustled River to the side and then went back and started talking with the man. His indignant expression faded as Tia turned on the charm, tossing her long red hair over her shoulder and flashing that beaming smile of hers.

River walked away, realizing her friend had just saved her from another reprimand from their boss.

You have to learn to deal with customers who come on to you in a polite manner, her manager would always say. *Simply say no, and if that doesn't work, excuse yourself and find another staff member or manager to step in.*

River knew the drill, but any guy who betrayed his girlfriend, or tried to bully a woman into doing something she didn't want to do, like go out with him, made her see red.

She walked to the break room door, watching while Tia chatted to the man.

"You had a little trouble, I see." Her manager, Louise, stepped up beside her.

"Tia took over," River said, a bit resentful that Louise had been watching her so closely. Waiting for her to make a mistake.

"I'm glad. I'd hate to write you up for being rude to a customer again." Louise glanced at River's hands. "I don't recognize the shade of nail polish you're wearing. It's not one of ours, is it?"

River curled her fingers. "No," she admitted.

"River, you know that everyone who works in the store is supposed to wear our nail polishes. Especially the new spring line."

River cringed inside. Normally, she loved the products the boutique carried, and often gave rave reviews on her blog—that's one of the reasons she'd wanted to work here in the first place—but the spring line was too ordinary for her. Soft pastels in a plain cream finish.

River liked some pizzazz on her nails. Bright colors or deep rich tones with multichrome flakies were her favorites. Maybe some flashy design in strong metallic tones. Or a leather finish with studs.

Cream pastels just didn't do it for her. So she'd worn one of her own creations, a duochrome that shifted from turquoise to a rich blue depending on how the light hit it.

"Make sure when you come in on Saturday that you're wearing one of the spring shades"—Louise raised her eyebrow—"or consider looking for a new job. Understand?"

"But I'm not supposed to be working on Saturday." River had already sent the e-mail confirming she would meet the person who'd paid so much to have dinner with her. She didn't want to jeopardize getting the investment. Starting her own nail polish company was her dream and if she didn't honor the dinner, she could lose that investment and the whole Kickstarter campaign would drop below the minimum and she wouldn't get anything.

"I changed the schedule. It's posted in the break room."

"Please, Louise, I have something else to do on Saturday. It's really important."

"Cancel it. I need you here." Then Louise turned and walked away.

"Tia, please. I'll take any shift you want. Just cover for me on Saturday."

"Sorry, Riv. I told you I'm going to my cousin's wedding. I mean really, I'd love to get out of it, but if I don't go, my mom'll kill me."

River sighed. "I get it. Sorry to be a bug."

"You've already asked everyone else?"

River nodded. She'd phoned everyone in the store over the past two days, but no one wanted to give up a Saturday off.

"Okay, look, move the dinner back to eight," Tia suggested. "Louise always takes off midafternoon and Wendy's closing that night. If you're lucky, it won't be too busy, so just ask Wendy if you can take off a little early. If you offer to work for her on a Sunday sometime, I'm sure she'll say okay."

She wasn't lucky. River glanced at her watch and it was already seven o'clock and she was still waiting for her customer to decide between Pink Fizz and Seafoam. River was almost ready to tell her to take both, one as a gift, and River would pay for it out of her own pocket, but finally the woman chose the Pink Fizz, the one she'd clearly favored all along, and took her purchases to the register.

Wendy hurried over as soon as she finished with her own customer. "Go ahead and take off. Sue and I can close up."

"Thanks, Wendy."

River headed to the break room and grabbed her purse. On the way through the store, the same customer stopped her.

"Excuse me, can you help me pick out one of these nail polish gift sets for my sister's birthday?" It seemed she'd left her purchases at the counter and was talking another look around.

Oh, God, River was already late.

"I can help you with that," Sue said, appearing from nowhere.

"Oh," the customer said. "Okay, thank you." She picked up two of the attractive boxes and showed them to Sue, who smiled and nodded.

River mouthed a thank you, then hurried out of the store.

As River approached the glass door of the restaurant, a woman in black pants, a crisp white shirt, tie, and red brocade vest opened the door from the inside and held it for her.

"Good evening," the woman said. "Welcome to the Carousel."

"Thank you." River was a little intimidated by the posh décor as she stepped inside. "I'm a little late for a reservation. It's in my name. River Cassidy."

"Of course, Ms. Cassidy. I'll take you to your table."

River followed the tall, elegant woman into the dimly lit restaurant, candles illuminating the intimate booths. They walked down a hallway, River presumed to another section, but the woman stopped in front of a door and knocked, then opened the door.

River followed her inside and realized it was a private dining room with a chandelier of candles over the table, a lovely floral arrangement on the table and . . .

Her heart stopped as she saw the man rising to his feet from one of two upholstered armchairs arranged by a corner fireplace.

"River. How nice to see you again."

Her chest clenched as she took in his chiseled jaw, full lips, perfectly proportioned nose, and mesmerizing indigo eyes.

She had hoped she'd *never* see Kane Winters again.

The sight of him triggered an array of painful memories. She remembered how sweet it had been to feel his arms around her, his lips brushing hers. His muscular body over hers. His cock driving into her and taking her to heaven.

And she remembered how he'd betrayed her . . . and humiliated her.

"You're nailpolishlover209?"

He smiled and walked toward her as the hostess exited, closing the door behind her.

"Yes, that's me."

"I'm not staying." She turned and reached for the door handle.

"You owe me dinner."

She frowned. "Order what you want. I'll leave my credit card number with the hostess."

"I don't care about that. What I want is to spend time with you." He smiled. "I would think I'd get more than sixty seconds for my five thousand dollars."

She turned around, fuming. "I don't want to spend time with *you*."

"But you will." He pulled out a chair, waiting for her to take a seat. "Because you always honor your word."

Anxiety coiled through her. He was right and they both knew it. She walked stiffly to the table and sat down. He guided the chair forward, then picked up the linen napkin that had been folded into a swan and shook it out, then handed it to her. He always had been quite the gentleman. She took the napkin, the brief contact of his fingers brushing hers sending sparks flashing along her nerve endings, throwing her wildly off balance.

He sat down across from her and placed his own napkin on his lap. She imagined the linen brushing over his thick, muscular thighs. Remembered what it felt like to have her legs wrapped around them.

"You know I never would have agreed to dinner if I'd known it was with you," she said.

"But you really have no choice. When you put out an offer like that, you have to take what you get."

"And I got you."

He smiled. "Yes."

He was far too pleased with himself and she hated it.

"Why would you spend *five thousand dollars* for an hour with me?"

His eyebrow arched. "It'll be at least three hours. You're staying for dessert and coffee." He lifted the bottle of wine and poured rich burgundy liquid into the crystal stemmed glass in front of her.

"I can eat faster than that."

"I'm sure you can. But they won't serve a five-course meal faster than that. And before you argue, I've already ordered."

"But that's too much food. I couldn't possibly—"

"The vichyssoise will be here in a moment and yes, you could possibly." He sipped his wine. "Look, you agreed to have dinner with me . . ."

"Not with you . . ."

"So why don't you just relax and enjoy it?"

A knock sounded, then the door opened. A waiter entered with a small tray, which he set on a side table, then placed a small bowl in front of her.

She realized the waiter had knocked because he'd wanted to warn them he was coming in . . . so he didn't interrupt anything. Her cheeks flushed at the thought the waiter might think that they'd be . . . doing something together.

He served Kane next, then set a basket of fresh baked rolls on the table. The aroma of the bread, still warm, made her mouth water.

She'd gone off grains a couple of weeks ago, but knew she would not be able to resist tonight. She took one, still warm to the touch, and cut it open, then smeared butter on it. It melted as she spread it. She took a bite and had to stop herself from sighing. She did *not* want Kane to know she was enjoying any part of this.

Kane watched River as she took a bite of the roll. The look of bliss on her face made him wish he was the one giving her so much pleasure.

And he would be. Of that he was sure. She was reluctant now, but he intended to make up for the pain he'd caused her in college and convince her that they could have a future together. It wouldn't be easy, but that had never stopped him from going after what he wanted before. A challenge made the victory all that much sweeter.

She dipped her spoon into the soup and tasted it. He could see her eyes light up. This place had the best vichyssoise he'd ever tasted. One of the reasons he'd chosen it. Though the most important reason was the private dining room.

She glanced at him, then schooled her expression to one of ambivalence.

He had to stop from chuckling. She'd always thought she could hide her emotions, but he'd always been able to read her like an open book.

The restaurant had provided Kane with a small buzzer that he'd put in his pocket. It allowed him to signal the staff with a push of a button when they were ready for the next course. It also meant they would be interrupted only when Kane signaled they were ready, which allowed him privacy to discuss his proposal with her after dinner.

He pushed the button and moments later, the waiter returned with their shrimp cocktail.

River had clearly decided that not talking was the best course of action, and he allowed her that option until after the salad.

When the main course arrived—chateaubriand and lobster tails, which he knew she loved—her eyes widened. He realized it was because she probably knew how much it cost. Knowing River—and he did—she would have looked up the menu online before she came and would know that the chateaubriand alone was into the three digits. Add the lobster and the other courses and the meal was probably close to a week's pay for her. That wasn't even counting the bottle of wine, which doubled that amount.

The waiter served the food from the beautiful platter onto their plates, then refilled their wineglasses. A moment later, he disappeared out the door.

Kane leaned forward. "River, don't worry about the cost of the meal. I'm paying for it."

Her wide blue gaze darted to his, looking thankful at first, then shifting to determined.

"No, it's my responsibility to pay for dinner."

"Actually, it doesn't say that anywhere in the agreement. So I believe it's my prerogative to pay if I choose."

"But—"

"If you insist on paying for dinner for me, then we can go to a roadhouse for a second dinner and we'll count this as a rehearsal dinner."

"A rehearsal dinner? It's not like we're getting married." Instantly her cheeks flushed a deep rose color.

He laughed. "Really? Talk of marriage so soon? We've barely gotten started renewing our connection. Give us a little time."

She practically growled. "We aren't renewing anything. Once this dinner is done, I'm gone and we never see each other again."

"Well, no, not really."

River's eyes narrowed as she stared at him suspiciously. "What do you mean?"

"I mean, I didn't just buy this dinner opportunity with you. Did you notice how quickly your campaign hit the target?"

"Yes," she said slowly, her stomach tightening. *Please, don't let him say that*—

"I bought all the options."

Oh, God, he'd said it.

"All of them?"

"That's right."

The superb taste of the chateaubriand soured in her mouth. She put down her fork and stared at him.

"What are you going to do with five hundred bottles of nail polish?"

The option rewards had basically been choices of nail polish. The lower-cost options included a single bottle of polish, the middle level included packages of the basic shades of the collection, and the high-level rewards were sets of the whole collection, which included the special top coats. Altogether, that would be about five hundred bottles.

Her heart sank. She'd been so happy that so many people would be trying her nail polish and hopefully love it and want to come back for more. She'd seen this as a way to grow her clientele. But because of what Kane had done, she'd reached only one client, and he didn't even care about the polish. He had just used this as an opportunity to trap her into seeing him again. Altogether the campaign had raised twelve thousand dollars, including this dinner, and after expenses—including the huge outreach to bloggers as she'd intended—she would be left with enough to buy more supplies and get a kick-ass Web site set up, and do some promotion, but without that base of clients . . .

He shrugged. "I don't know. Maybe I'll build a special room for them. I can have you come and organize them for me."

She quirked her eyebrow. "I don't think so."

"So how many nail polishes do you have?" he asked.

She shifted in her seat. "In stock, you mean?"

"No, I mean personally."

Oh, God, she didn't want to reveal her quirky obsessiveness. "Um . . . I have a few."

His grin broadened. "Come on. Tell me."

She pursed her lips. "Well . . . about . . . uh . . . fourteen hundred."

He chuckled.

"Why are you laughing?"

"Well, for someone who is tight for cash, that's a lot of money tied up. Each bottle is what . . . twenty-five dollars?"

Her eyes widened. "Are you kidding? Sure, a bottle of Louboutin goes for fifty dollars." She'd seen the stylish bottle online and drooled over the facet-shaped bottle that looked like a jewel and the tall slender cap, like one of the iconic stiletto heels from the designer's line of shoes. "Or Dior for thirty to forty dollars. Azature, which is infused with a crushed diamond, is twenty-five, but I only have one of those." Her one indulgence. "Most of what I have are two-dollar brands from the drugstore. Like Sinful Colors. They're really nice," she defended. She didn't mention that she did have several from the boutique where she worked, but with her store discount they weren't too pricey.

"Even at two dollars a bottle, that's close to three grand."

She leaned back in her chair, her back stiff. "Sure, but I don't have many shoes."

His eyes glittered and he laughed again, a deep, delightful sound. "What does that have to do with anything?"

"Well, I'm just saying. A lot of women buy lots of shoes. But I don't. And shoes are thirty or forty dollars a pair."

"Sweetheart, I have no idea where you shop, but the last pair of shoes I bought for a woman was over a thousand dollars."

She crossed her arms. "I think you just made my point."

She pushed aside her plate, her meal only half eaten. Under the covered silver platter on the side table, more food was being kept warm.

"Look, I don't want to argue about nail polish or shoes, or why we're here," she said. "I have to work tomorrow so I'd like to go home."

"There's still dessert."

"I'm full."

"Then stay for coffee."

"I—"

But he glanced at his gold Rolex watch and she sighed. "Fine."

He picked up his napkin and wiped his mouth, leaving his meal unfinished, then pulled back her chair. "Let's sit by the fireplace."

But when she stood up, he rested his hand on her upper arm—the action intimate and totally familiar—and her heart raced. She couldn't think with him this close. With him touching her like that.

Before she knew what was happening, he drew her close and his lips brushed hers. She sucked in a breath, immobile at the shock of his solid body against hers, her hormones swirling through her. Then his lips pressed more firmly, coaxing, and his tongue slipped inside her mouth. She melted against him, the deep, intense yearning she'd suffered so long . . . that she'd buried inside so deep she thought it would never resurface . . . stole away her reasons for keeping him at a distance. Denied her the barriers she needed to keep her sanity while in his arms, plucking each excuse from her brain before it could surface.

Chapter Two

The feel of River's soft body against him, her lips pliant under his, sent heat flooding to his groin. Kane wanted her more than he'd wanted any other woman. She had become an obsession he couldn't rid himself of. He'd tried. After what had happened between them at college, he knew that she would never forgive him, and he'd convinced himself it was for the best. For both of them. But she'd haunted his dreams. She'd become the woman he compared every other woman to . . . and they all came out lacking.

He wanted her more than he wanted anything.

And he'd decided he would have her.

The Kickstarter campaign had been a golden opportunity, practically custom made to help him.

And now here she was, melting against him.

He stroked his hands down her back until his fingers brushed the swell of her lovely ass, then he pulled her tight against him . . . and his hard, aching cock. Her lips tugged from his on a gasp, then she drew her hands from around his neck and pushed against his shoulders.

She turned away, clearly flustered.

"I really need to go."

"No, we have some business to discuss."

"There's no business. You bought some of my product, and the opportunity to have dinner with me tonight. That's all. Dinner is over. And I will send the nail polishes in four weeks."

"Four weeks? That's a long time for me to wait."

She turned back to him and quirked an eyebrow. "You're in a rush for them, are you?"

He smiled. "Personally, I could wait, but if you'd like them to be sold in Rapture, then I'll need them sooner than that."

River's eyes widened in shock.

Rapture was a boutique that specialized in designer products. Their very high-end clientele included actors, rock stars, multibillionaires.

"What are you talking about?"

Her heart pumped loudly. He couldn't really mean he'd made a deal with Rapture to carry *her* nail polish.

"Come and sit down so we can talk. The waiter will bring coffee and dessert."

"I told you I don't want dessert."

"So you'll just drink the coffee." He guided her to one of the chairs by the fireplace.

As she sat down, the waiter arrived with his now

familiar knock. Kane told him to leave the dessert—banana cream pie, which was her favorite—on the table. Then the waiter poured them each a cup of coffee, asking how she liked it. He added her cream and sugar and handed her the cup. After he served Kane, he set a bottle of liqueur on the low table between the chairs along with two small liqueur glasses, then poured the creamy liquid into them.

She couldn't resist Baileys and Kane knew it. She picked up her glass and sipped.

"The owner of Rapture is an old friend of mine, and when I explained to her that I'd found a talented new designer with a nail polish line, she was quite interested. I sent her a picture and a description of your collection and she asked for exclusive rights to distribute it."

"Exclusive rights—"

He held up his hand. "Don't worry. They have a guaranteed minimum order for a collection for all four seasons, plus a holiday collection. And exclusivity is only guaranteed for one year. After that you can continue the arrangement or choose to supply other stores. You can really go either way. With them you'll be established as a high-end product and can charge whatever you like for your polish. Probably in the thirty-to-fifty-dollar range. If you open up to other stores, you'll probably want to drop your price, or come out with a more affordable line for department stores, but keep a more exclusive line for Rapture."

Her heart was in palpitations and her breathing uneven. Here he was casually talking about her polish being sold by *Rapture* . . . and she was still getting over the shock that such a thing was even possible.

"I don't know how . . . I mean . . . they'll really carry my polishes?"

Kane's heart swelled at the sight of the subdued joy in her eyes. She blinked, clearly in disbelief.

He leaned forward and took her hand, pleased when she didn't jerk it away.

"Yes, River. They really will."

"But . . ."

He thought he saw tears shimmering in her eyes, but she blinked them back.

"Why did you do this?"

He compressed his lips. "I want to make up for what happened between us."

Now she snatched her hand from his, her head shaking. "You can't . . . this won't . . ."

He took her hand again, and held it tight enough she couldn't pull it away. "But it's a start."

She stared at him, uncertainty flickering in her eyes. He released her hand and she leaned back in her chair. She picked up her glass and finished the liqueur. As soon as she put it down, he refilled it.

"I'll have to work quickly," she said. "They want five hundred bottles?"

"Actually, seven hundred. For now. Then they want you to deliver another five hundred within a month after that."

"Seven hundred bottles," she said, her voice a little shaky. She stared at her hands, then nodded. "Okay. I'll get going on that. Thank heavens I already have three hundred ready to go." She raised her gaze to his. "I'll get it done."

"I know you will. And if there's anything I can do to help . . ."

She tipped her head. "You want to help mix nail polish and fill bottles?" she asked doubtfully.

He laughed. But in fact, the thought of spending countless hours working by her side, sleeves rolled up, helping her achieve her dream held a certain appeal. Especially the idea of being alone with her.

"I'm happy to do that, but there are more efficient ways I could be of use. Like supplying staff to help you get the work done."

She shook her head. "No, that would increase the expenses. I don't have enough up-front capital."

"It's not a problem if I pay for them."

She frowned. "Get this straight right now. I will not accept charity from you."

"Fair enough. But if I'm your partner, it's not charity."

"What? No. No way. You are not my partner."

He shrugged. "The only way to get the deal with Rapture is if I'm a partner. Francoise won't make a deal like this with an unknown entity. She knows me and knows if I'm involved, she has no worries about the product being delivered on time and being of the highest quality."

His heart ached at the disappointment etching her eyes.

Her hands clenched around the armrests and she

pushed herself to her feet. "Well, I should have known it was too good to be true." She started across the room. "Good night."

"River, wait. Are you really going to walk away from this deal for such a small thing?"

She spun around, glaring at him. "Small? Giving up control of my company to you?"

He stood and walked toward her. "Sweetheart, I'm not taking over your company."

"Don't call me sweetheart," she said through gritted teeth.

"I'll simply be an investor. You will control the company."

She planted her hands on her hips. "I don't believe you."

"Why would I want to run a nail polish company? Can't you just accept that I want to help you?"

"To pay me back for what you did? Well, that will never happen. It'll never be enough."

She continued to the door.

"River, just think about it. We can meet again in a couple of days."

She hesitated, her hand on the doorknob.

"Don't let your dream slip away. Meet me at Hades on Tuesday evening."

Hades was a trendy uptown bar. The irony wasn't lost on him that she would feel she was making a deal with the devil.

She sucked in a deep breath. "I'll think about it. But don't expect a yes."

"No worries there. I never know what to expect from you."

River got on the bus and took a seat near the middle doors. She stared out at the passing cars as the bus drove.

Why? Why did it have to be *him*?

At the memory of the embarrassment and humiliation he'd caused her so many years ago, heat rose to her cheeks. She'd been devastated. When he'd asked her out, she'd thought he'd actually been attracted to her . . . she'd definitely been attracted to him. But to him the whole thing had just been . . . nothing.

She should have known. Right from the beginning, her best friend had warned her. But she'd thought Luanne had just been overprotective and maybe even a little jealous. River and Luanne had both been those girls that nobody quite got. Quirky and a little too strange. Certainly not someone the most eligible, attractive guy at school would be interested in.

First year of college—Spring semester
River stared at the symbols in her chemistry textbook, brushing back her hair as the breeze fluttered it across her face. The sun shone brightly on this warm, spring afternoon. She'd rather be doing anything other than studying, but the final exam was tomorrow and chemistry was her worst subject. She had to ace it to keep her scholarship.

She breathed in deeply, the fragrance of the lilacs

tempting her to sit back and enjoy the sight of the campus around her. For a while, a few guys had been playing Frisbee on the grass beside her, but when a few of their friends joined them, they sat on the grass and chuckled then talked low amongst themselves. She ignored them, keeping her gaze on her book. They were probably rating the girls walking by.

She turned the page.

"Hey, studying for the exam tomorrow?"

She glanced up from her book to see Kane Winters standing by the bench. Her breath caught.

He was stunningly gorgeous, as usual. He wore dark denim jeans and a casual blue shirt with alternating darker and lighter blue stripes, and enough buttons open at the neck to give her a glimpse of his muscular chest. His dark hair was slightly longer than his friends' more close-cropped styles, yet combed neatly into place. The thick waves gleamed in the sunlight. And the smile he flashed her was heart-stopping.

His deep blue, almost purple eyes were locked on her and she felt . . . exposed.

He sat down beside her and she pushed herself straighter, her back stiffening. He'd never said a word to her before—in fact, she'd been sure he didn't even know she existed—yet now here he was, sitting beside her. Talking to her.

"Yeah. And you?" she asked.

Oh, God, that was stupid. Of course he wasn't studying. He'd just been sitting with his friends. And he always pulled off As in chemistry. And every other class she was in with him.

He shrugged. "I'll look over my notes tonight." Then he smiled. "If you'd like some help studying, maybe we could get together." He sent her a disarming smile, a definite glint in his indigo eyes. "Chemistry is my specialty."

The seductive tone in his voice sent tremors through her. She was pretty sure the chemistry he was talking about was not the same as in the textbook. God, was he actually coming on to her?

"I don't know . . ."

"We could grab some dinner first. There's this great place on Main. Donatello's. Know it?"

She frowned. "I can't afford a place like that."

"My treat."

"No, I'm sorry."

"Okay, we can just grab a pizza at this place called Stefano's on Kilburn, then go back to my place to study."

"I don't think so."

"Come on. You have to eat, right? And you're going to be studying anyway. Why not with me?"

Oh, God. She didn't understand this and she didn't think she wanted to. Because she feared if she did understand why this popular, sexy stud was talking to her—inviting her out—that she wouldn't like the reason.

She wanted to take him up on his offer. To live like someone who wasn't a misfit. To know what it felt like to be accepted.

And because she was wildly attracted to him. She had been from the moment she'd first set eyes on him in September on the first day of classes. But she'd known right then and there that he was someone she'd never get to know. Never date.

But now here he was, asking her out. How could she say no?

Then he flashed her that smile again and her barriers withered.

"Okay," she said.

"Great. I'll pick you up at five."

"No, it's okay. I'll meet you there. Five-thirty?"

"Sure."

He stood up and she watched him walk back to his friends. A few of them were chuckling and whispering amongst themselves, but when he returned, they got up and started tossing the Frisbee again.

By bus, it would take her at least forty-five minutes to get to Kilburn Street. Sometimes she cursed her own stubbornness at not accepting things from others.

She saw Luanne walking toward her, her gaze on the guys. She slumped into the seat beside River.

"What were you doing talking to him?" Her tone sounded accusing.

"I don't know. He just came over and invited me to study with him tonight."

"You're kidding, right?" Luanne said.

River shook her head.

"You're not going, are you?"

At River's silence, Luanne's brown eyes widened. "What the hell? Are you crazy?"

"He's good at chemistry and I could use the help."

"You don't really think he's interested in studying, do you?"

"Well, I doubt he wants to *do* anything with me. I'm not exactly his type."

"That's true. But it wouldn't stop him from having sex with you if he got the chance."

"What if that was okay with me?"

"It'll be okay with you if he nails you just to show he can? 'Cause maybe he's going slumming, or just wants some variety?"

"You're being pretty insulting, Luanne. You don't think he might actually like me?"

Luanne snorted. "Based on what evidence? Up 'til now you've been totally invisible to him."

River closed her textbook and pushed it into her backpack. Luanne could be insensitive and callous sometimes.

"I'm heading home."

When she stood up, Luanne grasped her arm. "Riv, just be careful, okay?"

River glanced at the concern in Luanne's brown eyes and nodded. Her friend was just looking out for her.

"Of course. I'll see you later."

River arrived at the restaurant at five-thirty to find that Kane had already ordered a pizza for them and a couple of sodas. She felt awkward as she sat down at the table across from him.

"I got the special," he said. "You aren't vegetarian, are you?"

She shook her head.

The waiter brought their pizza and set it on a metal stand.

Kane placed a slice on her plate, then one on his, then he took a bite.

She watched his full lips move as he ate. Desire coiled inside her at the thought of those lips moving on hers. Of his masculine hands gliding along her skin. Of him undressing her and . . .

"River?"

She snapped to attention as she realized he'd just said something.

"What?"

"Don't you want any pizza? I could get you something else."

"No, that's okay." She picked up a piece and bit into it. It was warm and cheesy, with a spicy flavor from the Italian sausage.

"So what do you plan to do when you graduate?" he asked.

She shrugged. Graduation was a long way off. "I'm not sure yet."

All she knew for certain was that she wanted a better future than her parents had offered. Her dad had been in and out of jail when she'd been growing up—she'd never known why—then finally her mom had left him. Her mom was an exotic dancer and worked until all hours of the night. River used to be afraid sleeping in the apartment all by herself, always relieved when she finally heard her mother come in at night.

Unless she'd had a man with her.

Kane raised an eyebrow. "No idea?"

"I'm taking a broad spectrum of classes to keep my options open. I like math but I also like art. I'm taking sciences to keep more avenues available, but I like physics better than chemistry."

"So you'll just figure it out as you go along?"

She nodded and took a sip of soda. "It's hard because the courses I like aren't very practical, but the ones that are practical don't interest me much."

He picked up another piece of pizza and put it on his plate. "What do you think is practical?"

"I don't know. Being an accountant . . . going into law."

"But you don't like those?"

She shook her head.

"I know you're taking at least one business course. What about that? An MBA will help you get a good job."

She glanced his way. He'd noticed she was in his business class, too?

"Sure, but I won't be going to graduate school."

She would have a hard enough time paying off the student loans for the expenses her scholarship didn't cover.

She pushed aside her plate. "What about you? You probably have it all planned out."

"Pretty much. I'll be getting an MBA, then I'll start my own company. A friend of mine who's in computer science has some great ideas. I have money in trust from my grandparents to start a business, so we'll be partnering to do a start-up."

River was sure he meant Will Anderson, a studious, almost nerdy guy so unlike the frat boys he usually hung around, yet they seemed to be best buddies. Will was in the one computer science class she took and he always pulled off As.

"I'd love to start my own company one day," she said.

He smiled. "I'm sure you will." He glanced at her plate. "You all finished?"

She nodded.

"Okay, I'll get them to pack up the rest of the pizza." He smiled, a glint in his indigo eyes. "Then we'll go back to my place."

Chapter Three

Present

River realized the bus was coming up to her stop. She'd almost missed it, caught up in her reverie. Damn it, she just wanted to forget all about Kane Winters . . . and she had. But now he'd dropped right back into her life. And this time she couldn't just walk away.

She had to be cautious. She wouldn't let her guard down.

This time, she wouldn't let him hurt her.

Kane sipped his coffee, waiting for the waiter to bring the bill. He wanted another chance with River, but clearly she was going to fight him every step of the way. He smiled, remembering her soft body pressed tight against him, her lips moving under his. His groin tightened. He intended to have her back in his bed and the challenge would just make his victory all the sweeter.

When he'd talked to her that first time back in college,

he'd been surprised. He hadn't known what he'd expected, but he'd found he really enjoyed talking to her. She'd been the quirky girl with the odd clothes and the hair streaked with bright pink. He'd thought she'd have odd ideas and a keep-away attitude, but she'd been warm and pleasant to talk to.

Before that, he hadn't realized she was broke—struggling to keep up with her expenses and maintaining her scholarship so she could afford to stay in school. Most of the people he knew had parents who provided every-thing they needed. Will was a notable exception, but he still had some help from his parents. River was different. He admired her courage and her determination to suc-ceed.

He'd noticed her long before that fateful spring day—she had a pretty face and an alluring figure—but she wasn't the kind of girl someone like him would hang out with. And she certainly wouldn't fit in with his friends or be accepted by his family looking the way she did. He hadn't really cared about that kind of thing except for the practical aspect that she'd be uncomfortable not fitting in, so why start something with her that was bound to end?

But that day, he'd been challenged. And he'd found the challenge to be well worth the effort.

First year of college—Spring semester
Kane opened his apartment door and led River inside. Her eyes widened.

"Wow." She glanced around his place, taking in the clean lines of his contemporary black wood furniture, his sixty-inch plasma TV, the white leather furniture, and colorful art on the walls.

"Is this your parents' place?" she asked.

"No, this is my place." He tossed his keys in the drawer of the bureau in the entryway then walked into the living room. "Do you live in the dorms?"

She shook her head. "I rent a room in a house off campus."

He raised an eyebrow. "Wouldn't it be easier to live on campus?"

"Sure, but . . . I can't afford that."

Her answer confused him. He wouldn't want to live in the cramped, crowded dorms, but he thought living on campus was the cheaper alternative to off-campus housing . . . yet she couldn't even afford that.

"Would you like something to drink? I've got wine, beer, hard lemonade?"

"Lemonade, thanks."

He walked into the kitchen and retrieved a can of hard lemonade from the fridge, and poured it into a glass with ice, then grabbed a beer for himself. When he walked back into the living room, she was sitting on the couch with her chemistry textbook lying on the table.

She really had come over to study.

She took the drink he offered and sipped it, then frowned and pushed it aside as she opened her book.

For the next two hours, he went over the chapters with

her, reviewing and querying her to test her knowledge. The whole time he was aware of her closeness . . . her warmth . . . the sweet vanilla scent of her hair and the curve of her body.

"Let's take a break," he said.

"But we still have another chapter to go over."

"I know. We can do that after." He stood up and walked to the kitchen, then returned with another drink for each of them.

He set her lemonade in front of her, then sat down again.

"There's a party after the exam tomorrow. Would you like to go with me?"

"I'm not much for parties."

"But it's your last exam. You want to celebrate, don't you?"

She frowned. "I don't get it. Why are you asking me? Why did you even start talking to me today?"

A barrier had gone up and he feared he'd lose his chance with her.

He smiled. "Why are you so surprised that I want to go out with you?"

She stared at her glass. "I'm not like the girls you usually go out with."

"Maybe that's part of the attraction."

And he *was* attracted to her. Much to his surprise. While they'd been studying, whenever he explained something in the textbook, she'd leaned in closer to see the page and every brush of her thigh against his sent heat to his groin. Whenever she'd stroked her hair behind her ear, he'd wanted to brush his fingers through the soft strands . . . to feel her soft skin under his fingertips.

Her gaze locked on his, her green eyes serious.

"Are you slumming it with me? Getting some kind of strange kick from asking out the weird chick?"

A prickle of anxiety emanated from her and he wanted to quell her unease.

"You're different, that's true, but that's a good thing." He sent her his most disarming smile. "I really like you."

The barrier seemed to fade and she looked uncertain. Vulnerable.

He leaned forward and her eyes widened, but he could see the look of longing in them. This attraction he felt for her seemed to be mutual.

He closed the distance and brushed his lips against hers. Instead of pulling away, she leaned into the kiss. Then her mouth moved on his and heat blasted through him. Her tongue brushed against his lips and he opened them, drawing it into his mouth. Intoxicated by the sweetness of her.

He wrapped his arms around her and drew her tight to his body. Her soft breasts crushed against him and— God help him—he could feel her nipples harden through her shirt. His hand glided up her side, then he cupped her soft breast.

She stiffened and jolted back, sucking in a breath. She shook her head, looking panic-stricken.

"No, I can't . . ." She was on her feet and racing for the door.

He stood up and strode after her, scooping up her backpack on the way.

She reached the entrance and grabbed the doorknob, but he grasped her arm before she could open the door.

"Wait. Let's talk . . ."

Her head jerked around and she stared up at him, her eyes wide with . . . damn, was that fear?

She backed against the door as if seeking escape.

"No, I . . . need to go home."

"River, I'm sorry. I didn't mean anything. You seemed to be enjoying the kiss and—"

"No!" she flared. "I didn't want you to do that. It's not my fault."

"River . . ." He said her name in a calm, soothing voice as he drew her back from the door. This wasn't a conversation for the neighbors. "I'm not saying it was your fault. I just misread the situation. I shouldn't have touched you like that. I'm sorry."

She was breathing quickly and his chest tightened.

"Do you want to talk about it?" he asked.

She shook her head. "I just want to go home."

"Okay. I'll drive you."

"No, I'll take the bus."

He pulled his keys from the bureau drawer. "I'm going to drive you."

She glanced at him uncertainly as he drew her gently from the door and opened it.

"I just want to ensure you get home safely. Okay?"

She bit her lip, then finally nodded and stepped through the door.

It was clear something had happened to her in the past. Something that had scarred her deeply. And, God damn it, he wanted to kill the bastard who'd done it.

Present

The waiter arrived with the bill and Kane paid.

"Do me a favor and pack up the pie and have it sent to the young lady." He handed him an extra twenty.

"Of course, sir."

Kane scribbled her name and address on the back of his business card and handed it to the man, then left the restaurant.

The memory of her pain that night still haunted him, and what had happened the next day had scarred her even more.

Because of him.

And he intended to make up for it somehow.

River stashed her purse in the locker at Giselle's, feeling tired and cranky. She hadn't slept well last night—of course she hadn't after seeing Kane again. She was appalled at herself for the desire she had felt for him when he'd kissed her. For the fact she'd wanted that kiss . . . and more.

He had hurt and betrayed her in college and she couldn't let go of that pain. She couldn't trust him.

She went to the register as Louise unlocked the door.

There were already customers waiting to come in. The big electronics store in the mall was having a huge sale that day with hourly specials and it looked like a lot of wives and girlfriends weren't as interested in wireless routers.

The morning was fast and furious and River wound up selling more in those few hours than she'd sold all week. She thanked her current customer as she handed the woman her bag and realized there was no one else waiting.

"River." Louise stepped beside her, a frown on her face. "You didn't ask her to sign up for our text promotion."

Aw, damn.

"Sorry, Louise, I—"

"In fact, you haven't signed up a single person today."

"It was really busy and—"

"That's no excuse. It's a new promotion and management wants us signing up as many people as possible." She glared at River. "They feel it will increase business."

"But most people I ask are already signed up for e-mail coupons."

Louise tapped her nails on the glass counter impatiently. "I want you to sign up at least five new people this afternoon. Understood?"

River drew in a breath. "Yes."

She realized that Louise was staring critically at her nails. Now what was wrong? She'd put on one of the spring colors. She'd chosen Blue Me Away, which was a soft periwinkle. She glanced down at her nails. Oh, God, there was a big chip in the polish, revealing naked nail on her index finger. And another on her thumb.

"Do you really think it's appropriate for your nails to be in such a state? It doesn't leave a very good impression on the customers. Would you buy nail polish from someone who doesn't even know how to take care of her own nails?"

River had to bite back a sharp retort. River knew how to take care of her nails and she also knew a decent polish when she used one. This polish was gloppy and applied unevenly. And it clearly didn't last, since she'd put it on only two days ago, and used a quality base coat and top coat. *Her* nail polish didn't chip after only two days' wear. Ever.

By break time, River had signed up two people for the text program.

"How you doing?" Tia asked when they sat down for a quick coffee at the Starbucks in the mall. Tia had come on shift at noon. "It seems like Louise has been giving you a hard time."

River stared at her nails. She'd done a quick fix by applying White Water, Pink Fizz, and Seafoam over the blue polish in quick strokes using an almost dry brush, giving her nails a sort of grunge multicolored effect. Louise had raised her eyebrow with a critical glare, but River had been with a customer at the time, so Louise hadn't said anything. River couldn't help feeling a little smug when the customer called her friend over and asked River to show them how she'd done it. Especially when that resulted in a sale of all four colors to each of them.

"Nothing new there. Louise clearly doesn't like me."

"Oh, well. Screw her. The customers like you. And anyway, you're going to start your own business and a year from now, you'll be laughing at us poor saps who have to drag our asses in to someone else's business and follow their rules." Tia patted River's hand. "You'll be making your own rules."

Her own rules. Yeah, not if Kane got his way.

"You know that a start-up company like mine probably won't even be profitable in a year. I'll still be schlepping into the store with you."

"Naw. You're going to be a big success. I know it. You're talented and smart."

"Not that smart. I didn't even finish college."

"That doesn't matter. You're going to make it big. I know you are." Tia squeezed her hand. "I believe in you."

The gesture filled River with warmth. She loved that Tia believed in her. And cared about her. She was just a casual friend—River didn't really get close to people—but Tia filled a void in her life. Tia cared about what happened to River more than her mother ever had. And her father had been practically nonexistent in her life.

"I know you do. Thanks." River smiled awkwardly. She patted Tia's hand, then drew hers away, unwilling to allow herself more of the comforting contact.

Tia sipped her coffee. "So how did dinner go with your Kickstarter person? Was she nice?"

River frowned. "She was a he."

"Oh?" She glanced at River. "You don't seem happy. Did he hit on you?"

"No." She certainly wouldn't tell Tia about the kiss. "He was a guy I knew in college."

"Oh? A guy you *dated* in college?"

She shrugged. "Do you consider going out two times dating?"

"That depends. Did you have sex with him?"

"Tia!"

Tia laughed. "I'm just kidding. I know you well enough to know that that would never happen. So what's the deal?"

Oh, God, if Tia only knew.

"He did something that . . . hurt me."

Tia's eyes filled with concern. "Oh, God. What, honey?"

River just shook her head. Tia knew how private River was, so she didn't push.

"Okay, well, it's over now. You don't have to see the jerk again."

"The problem is I'm not sure about that."

"You aren't? But why would you even consider it?"

River explained the whole thing about the deal with Rapture.

"Oh, wow. Yeah, that is a tough one. I don't know how you can turn something like that down." Tia stared at River. "If you want, I'll go with you when you meet him."

The rest of the afternoon whizzed by for River, with a constant flow of customers. Luckily, she got more than five people to sign up for the text program, so Louise gave her no more grief. By four o'clock when she went off shift, she was exhausted. She said good-bye to Tia, then just headed to the food court for something to eat, too tired to face making something at home.

"Hey, you're not having dinner with your boyfriend?"

She glanced up from her tray of food to see the guy who'd hit on her in the store the other day standing beside her in line. Her heart started to pound.

"Not tonight."

"Well, instead of eating that crap, why not join me for dinner? We could go out for Italian."

"No, thank you." Her hands balled into fists in her lap.

Some guys just didn't get the message.

He scowled. "You really are a bitch."

She stared at his back as he strode away, trying to calm her breathing. She'd learned to hold her ground, but confrontations like that always triggered memories of her mother's male friends. They would leer at her and . . . sometimes more . . .

A shiver rippled through her, but she pushed away the memories.

She ripped open the catsup package and squeezed out a red puddle onto her cheeseburger wrapper, then dipped in a fry.

Kane had never filled her with apprehension like most men did. That one incident . . . she'd been reacting to the situation, not him.

Go figure. The one man she'd let her guard down with had done the most damage.

First year of college—Spring semester
River walked out of the chemistry exam drained. She was a good student, but she found exams intimidating and stressful. It was seven p.m. and all she wanted to do was go back to her room and crash.

Then she saw Kane walking toward her.

"Hi. How did you do?" he asked.

She nodded. "Okay, I think. Thanks." She kept walking.

He fell into stride beside her. "I wanted to talk to you about last night. I wanted to say I'm sorry again."

"Thanks." She kept walking, hoping he'd get the hint and move on.

"I was really hoping you'd come to the party with me tonight."

"I told you last night—"

"I know you did, but you were mad, and I understand why, but I was hoping you would change your mind." He took her hand and drew her to a stop. "Look, I'm not a bad guy. Won't you give me another chance?"

Then he gave her that heart-stopping smile of his. She couldn't help but stare into his indigo eyes and was struck by the sincerity she saw there.

She shook her head. "I'm really tired . . ."

"That's probably just low blood sugar. You'll have a

slice of pizza at the party and be as good as new." His smile broadened. "Really. You're not going to let me go there without a date, are you? Think of my reputation."

She couldn't help smiling. She knew as well as he did that no one would care if he had a date or not. Even if bringing a date was important, which it wasn't, he could get any girl he wanted. Anytime.

But for some reason, right now he wanted her.

"Okay, maybe I'll go for an hour or so."

"Great." Then he linked his hand with hers, sending her heart into delightful palpitations.

She walked with him to his car.

"If we'll be drinking, shouldn't we take the bus?" she asked.

"The party's near my place, so I'll drive to my apartment and we can walk from there."

Once they reached his apartment, they walked a couple of blocks through a nice neighborhood to an old but impressive brick house with a large yard, and loud music blaring from inside. She could barely believe students lived in this neighborhood, but then Kane's friends all came from money.

They went inside and clearly the party had been going on for a while. Kane led her to the kitchen and sure enough, there were boxes of pizza on the counter. She was starving, since she hadn't wanted to eat much before the exam. He gave her a large slice on a paper plate and she took a big bite while he grabbed her a vodka cooler and poured it over ice.

She sipped as she watched all the people around them. She recognized a lot of the faces, though they weren't people she'd ever talked to. A lot of people glanced their way, staring at her as if she didn't belong . . . and surprised to see her with Kane. But Kane didn't seem to notice.

"Hey, Will." Kane waved to his friend, a tall, sandy-haired guy in a black T-shirt sporting a depiction of an Escher painting. The one with the stairway without end. He glanced their way and smiled, then walked toward them.

"Will, this is River." Kane said.

"Hi. We're in the same computer-science class," Will said.

Unlike the stereotypical computer nerd, who was a small, geeky guy with glasses, Will was broad-shouldered, very muscular, and quite handsome. And his insightful hazel eyes seemed to see right into her soul.

He took her hand and shook it. The warmth of his fingers around hers was . . . nice.

"That's right," she said, a bit timidly. She was surprised he'd noticed her. And she was a little taken aback at his warmth and genuine smile.

"I was telling River that you and I plan to start a business together after graduation," Kane said.

"Yeah, if I can ever actually graduate."

"You two go back a long way?" she asked.

"Actually, no," Will said. "We met here in September, but hit it off. Kane's not usually the type of guy I hang with. Too stuck up."

"Thanks, man."

Will laughed. "But I put up with him."

"Yeah, anyway. This guy's brilliant when it comes to anything to do with technology."

"So why are you worried about graduating?" she asked Will.

"He's not worried so much as having scheduling issues. His minor is Japanese and the classes are only offered as a full-year credit, but that doesn't tie in with his co-op placement, which is every four months starting in second year."

"You speak Japanese?"

"No, but I want to. So much of our culture is affected by manga, anime, video games developed in Japan—"

"Oh, God, don't get him started."

"Hey, Kane . . . Will . . . what the fuck?" Three guys ambled in their direction, the one talking clearly drunk. "There are chicks crawling all over the place . . . and I mean falling-down-drunk crawling. What are you boys doing out here when there are woman to get laid?"

"Ya mean to lay," one of his buddies said. "Or get laid by." Then he started laughing as if he'd told a hilarious joke.

"Hank, I'm with someone," Kane said.

Hank, the one who'd spoken first, frowned and gazed in River's direction.

"What? You're with the pink-haired freak?"

Chapter Four

River's chest constricted and she wanted to crawl under the table. At the same time, she noticed anger flare in Kane's eyes and he leaned forward slightly, as if ready to surge to his feet.

"Hey, Hank," Will interjected. "Why don't you guys show me where the keg is? I just got here."

Hank, whose face had gone pale, dragged his uncertain gaze from Kane's ferocious stare.

"Yeah, sure, man. It's out on the deck." Hank and his two friends headed across the kitchen toward the door leading outside.

"Nice meeting you, River," Will said with a warm smile, shaking her hand again. Then he turned and followed the others.

"Sorry about those jerks," Kane said. "I would have slugged him, but it wouldn't be a fair fight in his condition. And I don't think you're the type to be impressed by violence."

"True." But a part of her wished he'd done something to stand up for her.

As they finished their pizza, she felt all the more conspicuous. People came and went, passing through the kitchen to the deck to get refills from the keg and it seemed everyone glanced their way. At the pink-haired freak with popular Kane. A trio of girls passed by, giggling and glancing at her.

She started to fidget, wishing she was anywhere but here.

"Finished?" Kane asked.

She nodded and he took her hand and led her through the crowded kitchen into the living room. People were everywhere, chatting, dancing, laughing. River wasn't used to parties and found it loud and overwhelming. Kane must have sensed her discomfort because he led her down a hallway, then opened a door. Inside was a pool table and an air hockey table. Four guys were playing air hockey, but the pool table was free.

Kane picked up two pool cues from the rack on the wall and handed her one.

"Do you play?" he asked.

"No, I've never really had the chance."

He placed the white ball on the table and took the first shot, dispersing the balls. He took her hand and drew her to the side of the table near the white ball, then positioned himself behind her, telling her how best to take the shot. Then his arms came around her so he could help her line it up. But the heady scent of his aftershave filled her nostrils, and the warmth of his body so close, and the feel of his arms entwining with hers, made her knees weak. He helped her take the shot, keeping her steady. She sank one ball.

He helped her with the next few shots, until she got the hang of it, but she found herself longing for him to back her up against the table and lift her onto it, then step between her thighs and . . .

Oh, God, why was she thinking like that? She'd never . . . ever . . . She drew in a breath as he moved away after her shot.

The thought of being with a man, after the leering creeps who had been with her mother . . . after the time one of them cornered River and started touching her in ways that made her sick with revulsion . . . She'd just never wanted to. But with Kane . . . Oh, God, with him she could imagine letting go. Opening to him. Letting the flame of desire he'd ignited inside her flare to a blazing maelstrom.

He won the first game and the second, too, but she was improving. Other people had come in to play so they handed off their cues and walked into the hallway.

"You did great," Kane said, holding her hand as they walked through the house. "In no time you'll be pool shark."

She laughed. "Not likely. Especially since this is the last time I'll probably be near a pool table for quite a while."

He stopped and turned her to him. "There's a pool table in my apartment building." He smiled. "We could play whenever you like."

She gazed into his deep blue eyes. Was he really say-ing that . . . ? He expected to keep seeing her?

Then he leaned in and kissed her. His arms slid around her waist and he drew her close to his warm body, his lips moving softly on hers. All the noise . . . all the people . . . dissolved away. All that was real to her were his lips mov-ing on hers. His body pressed tight to hers.

Then their lips parted and he smiled. "Why don't we go outside and get some fresh air?"

She trailed after him, clinging tightly to his hand as he led her through the swarm of people until they reached a patio door. There was a big deck that wrapped around the house. She could hear a lot of people around the cor-ner, off the kitchen where the keg was. He led her down the steps to the yard. It was a clear night and in the moon-light she noticed the lovely gardens.

"Hey, Kane." A few girls were sitting on a bench with plastic cups in their hands.

He waved, but led her toward the back gate, which was open. They stepped through to a lovely park beyond.

He smiled. "It's a little quieter here."

She nodded, delighted to be alone with him. They walked along the moonlit path, then he drew her to the side, under a large tree, and gently backed her against the trunk. He gazed down at her, his eyes glittering, and stroked her hair behind her ear. The brush of his fingers sent tremors through her and she longed to feel his lips on hers again.

He leaned in and she tilted her face up, anticipating

his kiss. Their lips met and her pulse quickened. Her hands slid up his chest to his broad shoulders and around his neck. His mouth moved on hers in a gentle persuasion, then his tongue glided inside, stroking. His solid body pressed her against the bark of the tree and she leaned into him more, wanting this closeness. Loving the feel of his strong arms around her.

When their lips parted, he smiled, his eyes twinkling. He started to lean in for another kiss when they heard voices. His lips brushed hers again but she was nervous, knowing if others had walked into the park, they'd see her and Kane.

"Hey, Winters, gettin' lucky?" said one guy.

She cringed, clinging to Kane as she peered around him at the three guys walking toward them.

"Yeah, but it can't be much of a challenge," said a different guy. "A freak like her is probably hard up."

Oh, God. Her cheeks flushed and shame consumed her. How stupid she'd been to believe that she could ever have anything real with someone like Kane. He released her and turned around.

"Why don't you guys get lost?"

She ducked around the tree and strode across the park while Kane was distracted by the three guys. She didn't hear anything they said over the pounding in her ears. All she knew was that she had to get away from here right now. Away from them.

And away from Kane.

"Hey, River." Kane was racing after her.

She felt a hand grasp her arm and she tore it away.

Kane caught up and strode along beside her.

"Are you okay?" he asked, his words etched with concern.

Then she realized tears were flowing from her eyes and she dashed them away, hoping he wouldn't notice.

"Ah, damn. River, please stop."

This time when he wrapped his hand around her arm, she didn't pull away, but she didn't turn toward him, keeping her head down so he wouldn't see her red eyes.

"Those guys are jerks. I'm sorry what they said hurt you."

"Why are you spending time with someone like me?" Her words came out thin and coarse.

"What do you mean someone like you? I find you—"

She raised her head and glared at him, her anxiety turning to anger.

"My family is nothing like yours. I don't have any of the things your friends do."

He frowned. "It don't care about that."

"Really?" She crossed her arms over her chest. "And you wouldn't care that my father was a drug addict . . . or that he was in prison?" she challenged.

"Was he?"

"Yes."

To his credit, his expression didn't change. "I still don't care."

"And my mother? Want to know what she does for a

living?" Before he could respond, she said, "She's an exotic dancer."

River couldn't admit to any more. Not even to herself. She couldn't face believing that those men her mother had brought home . . . with River in the next room . . . were any more than dates. Or one-night stands. Or whatever. Surely her mother hadn't taken money for . . .

"River, I mean it. It doesn't matter." He placed his hands on her shoulders and turned her to face him. "I told you, I like you. And who your parents are or what they've done has nothing to do with that."

"I don't understand."

Most people, when they found out about her background, would have nothing more to do with her. When she and her mother had first moved to Ancaster, River had started making friends, but then when people found out . . . she'd become an outcast.

It had been a lonely existence and she'd been happy to move to a new town for college where no one knew her past. Now . . . oh, God . . . Kane already knew she didn't fit in with the rich kids. Why had she told him the sordid details about her family? She kicked herself for saying too much.

He drew her closer and stared at her, his eyes filled with concern.

"River, I feel badly for what you must have gone through when you were growing up. It must have been hard."

"I don't need your pity," she said in a tight voice, refusing to look at him.

"It's not pity. It's compassion." He stroked a tear from her cheek. "I wish I had been there to help you through it."

Her chest was so tight she could barely breathe, and her throat so closed she thought she'd choke. But the feel of Kane so close . . . the echo of his accepting words seeping through her . . . She drew in a deep breath.

"Thank you."

He squeezed her shoulders. "Of course. I just want to help."

His hands slid down her arms, then he took her hand and interlaced his fingers with hers. He drew her back to the path.

"You really don't care?"

He laughed. "I really don't."

She believed him. And she wanted to hug him . . . tight . . . and never let him go. She'd always lived with the stigma of her parents' behavior. With being judged by others. But knowing Kane accepted her, despite where she'd come from made her feel . . . special.

Well, not special really, but normal. Not an outcast. At least, not in his eyes.

And right now, that's all she cared about.

She walked alongside him, a little giddy . . . as if a huge weight had been lifted from her shoulders.

"Where are we going?" she asked, a grin creeping across her face.

"Where would you like to go?"

She glanced at his profile as they walked from the park to the sidewalk.

"How about your place?"

He glanced her way. "Really?"

"I believe what you told me last night . . . That you didn't mean to push me."

He had been sweet and caring, just as he was being tonight. He'd taken her home and had obviously been concerned about her. He'd even called her later to ensure she was okay.

"And we'll just talk, right? And hang out?"

He smiled. "Of course."

He squeezed her hand and she felt like she was walking on air. As they approached his building, she realized she wanted more, though. She didn't want to be afraid of being alone with a man. Of what he might do. Kane was the first man she had ever really trusted, and that kind of trust was new to her, but . . . it meant something.

In fact, it meant more to her than she could have ever imagined.

He unlocked the front door and opened it for her. A moment later, the elevator doors closed behind them and he pressed the button for the twelfth floor. As the elevator glided upward, an uncontrollable urge swelled through her and she turned to face him, then gazed into his eyes. They darkened as he watched her. She leaned in and he met her halfway, their lips merging.

The kiss turned passionate, desire surging through her like a tidal wave.

She wanted him. She'd never wanted a man before . . . had always been repelled by the very idea . . . but not with him. The need reached down into the core of her and blasted through her very being.

She needed to be with him.

And why not? He made her feel like a normal woman for the first time in her life and normal was good. Normal was what she wanted to be.

And normal women her age weren't virgins.

At least, not according to anyone she'd ever talked to.

Their lips parted and he gazed at her uncertainly. She took his mouth again, gliding her tongue between his lips. He groaned, and tightened his arms around her.

He released her lips and said breathlessly, "I thought we were just going to talk and hang out."

She grinned. "We can do that."

She grabbed a handful of his shirt and pulled him forward, capturing his lips again. Passion flared between them and when the doors whooshed open, they were both breathing heavily.

"Or we could do something much more fun."

He laughed as she grasped his hand and led him out of the elevator. She tugged him down the hall with her.

Yes, she fully intended to lose her virginity tonight. With Kane.

Present

Kane walked into his office and set his steaming mug of coffee on his desk. Sunshine streamed in the windows on this beautiful spring morning as he started up his computer.

"Good morning," Will said as he walked into the office and sat down across from Kane. He sipped his coffee and set it on Kane's desk. "So how did things go on Saturday?"

"Fine, thanks for asking. How about you?"

"Come on, man. Spill. How did your little venture go with River? Is she going to go for the partnership?"

Just as they'd planned in college, Will had become Kane's partner and he knew all about Kane's guilt over what had happened with River in college. Kane had been an insensitive fool and he should have done something at the time. Especially when he'd found out River had dropped out of school. But he hadn't known where to find her.

Not that he'd really tried. And to be honest with himself, a part of him had held back because, as much as he didn't judge her for her parentage, he knew that she would always strain against normal social expectations, which would make it very difficult for her to fit into his life. He'd told himself he was doing it for her, so she wouldn't be hurt by others' judgments of her, but deep inside he knew it was also because he wasn't willing to take on the challenge of those same judgments.

So he'd let her go.

He'd grown a lot since then.

He wondered how she'd changed since he knew her last. The hair she sported was closer to normal than her previous fuchsia streaks, now a deep burgundy. And she'd actually worn a soft pastel nail polish rather than something garish.

Had she mellowed since college, or was she trying harder to fit in? He'd find out if only she'd give him a chance. And that was a big if.

"I don't know, but I intend to convince her any way I can."

Will sipped his coffee as he stared at Kane with his insightful hazel eyes, assessing. Something Kane had become used to.

Will set down his cup. "Look, I get that you want to make it up to her, but you know you need to give her space. If she decides she doesn't want anything to do with you, you have to respect that."

Kane knew Will was on his side. There was no doubt in his mind. It had actually been Will who had found her Kickstarter campaign and alerted Kane to it. Kane knew that Will felt some level of responsibility for what had happened in college, too.

Kane raised an eyebrow. "Have we met?"

Will chuckled. "Yeah, I know."

They both knew that when Kane set his mind to something, he got it. That was fact.

"Just be careful you don't make matters worse," Will said.

It was a fair comment. Almost everything Kane had done with River had gone from bad to worse.

But Kane fully believed that there was nothing he could do that would make matters worse than they already were.

First year of college—Spring semester

Kane's pulse rose as River led him down the hallway. Her behavior in the elevator had his cock aching. After last night, he never would have imagined she would be willing to come back to his place again, let alone suggest what he believed she was suggesting now. But her passionate kisses and her eagerness to get to his apartment made it pretty clear.

He was going to get lucky tonight.

They reached his door and he pushed the key into the lock and turned it. As soon as they were inside with the door closed behind them, she pushed him back against it and kissed him again, her lips soft and insistent.

God, her assertiveness was fucking sexy.

He couldn't take it anymore. He wrapped his arms around her and turned her until he had her pressed against the wall, then he drove his tongue into her mouth. His hands glided down her sides, over the flare of her hips, then back up. He felt the swell of her breasts against his fingertips, sending heat flooding to his groin, and glided forward to cup one luscious mound . . . then stopped.

Chapter Five

Memories of last night . . . of how River had panicked . . . plagued Kane.

He tore his mouth from hers. "River, last night—"

She shook her head. "No, don't worry about last night. I want this. I want to be with you."

God, he couldn't resist. He cupped her soft breast. Immediately, her breath caught, and he saw a spark of anxiety in her eyes. He pulled back.

"River . . . ?"

She shook her head, her eyes wide and pleading. "I'm sorry. I'm not too good at this, and I am a bit nervous, but . . ." She pressed her hand to his cheek. "I really do want to do this with you. If you could just move slowly and be patient . . ." She bit her lip.

Okay, so she wasn't very experienced. He could do what she asked.

"Of course I'll be patient. And I'll go as slow as you want me to."

She nodded and smiled shyly. "Thank you."

He took her hand and led her to the couch.

As soon as she sat down, he said, "I'll be right back."

He went to the cabinet where he kept a small selection of wine and grabbed a bottle and a couple of glasses then turned on some soft music. He poured her a glass of wine and handed it to her.

He sat down beside her and lifted his glass. "To us."

Then in a corny gesture, he linked arms with her and they both took a sip.

He set his glass down. She took another sip. Then another as she watched him.

"I'm not trying to get you drunk," he said.

She sipped again, and put her glass on the table. "I know. It'll just help me relax."

"I don't know," he said with a smile, sliding his arm around her waist and drawing her closer. "We seem to be working at cross purposes, because I plan to get you *excited*."

She grinned and leaned against him. "Oh, I think we're on the same page."

Then she nuzzled his neck. Heat washed through him as her fingers played over his shirt and he realized she was undoing the buttons. Her hand glided down his chest as the shirt opened.

He pulled the shirt off and tossed it aside. She leaned forward and her soft lips pressed against his skin. She kissed across his chest then—Damn! His cock jolted to attention as she lapped at his nipple, then sucked. He glanced down

as her neon-green-tipped fingers found his other nipple—
which was hard as a bead—and toyed with it.

God, he wanted to touch her, but he wasn't quite sure
how to do that without spooking her. She leaned back and
unfastened the small buckles holding her black vest closed.
She shed the garment, grabbed the hem of her bright,
multicolored T-shirt, and pulled it over her head. Underneath she wore a simple bra, but it was black and lifted her
breasts nicely. And her breasts were larger than he had
imagined. He'd had a hint of their size last night with the
brief touch, but her clothing certainly hid their fullness.

He couldn't drag his gaze from them. When she
reached behind to unfasten the bra, his breath held. She
drew the straps from her shoulders, and with a blush on
her cheeks, she slowly drew the garment away.

He stared at her naked breasts, so full and round . . .
the nipples a deep dusky rose . . . swelling under his gaze.
He wanted to touch them so badly. His cock ached with
need. But he made no move.

She gazed at him uncertainly, then finally reached for
his hand and, to his delight, pressed it to her warm flesh,
her hard nipple pushing into his palm. He tightened his
fingers around her, cupping her in his hand.

"Your breasts are so beautiful," he said in awe.

He caressed the other one, loving the soft fullness in
his hand. And the silky feel of her skin.

She stroked her hands up the sides of his neck. Then
cupped his jaw and kissed him. Her lips hesitant on his.
He slid one arm around her waist and pulled her closer.

She shifted onto her knees and pressed tighter against him. Her tongue glided into his mouth, then led his back into hers, then she sucked.

He groaned and turned her, pressing her back onto the couch, then he prowled over her. He dragged his mouth from hers, and stared down at her perfect breasts. He lowered his head and captured one puckered nipple in his mouth. He suckled and she moaned, her hands curling around his head, her fingers threading through his hair.

He reached for her other nipple and stroked it, then rolled the hard bead between his fingertips. Then he switched. She arched against him.

He ran his hand down her flat stomach and found her jeans, then unfastened the metal button. He couldn't find the zipper, and realized there was another button, then another. He undid them all, and slid his hand inside the denim. He felt her soft skin, then her silky curls.

All the women he'd been with were either totally bare, or had just a small patch or strip of hair, but she seemed to be untouched. As he stroked, he realized she'd stopped moving and he glanced at her face.

"Are you okay?" he asked.

She just nodded, but then stroked down his stomach. Her fingers stopped at the waistband of his jeans. He unfastened them and drew out his cock. Her eyes widened then she slowly reached for him and wrapped her hand around him.

God, the feel of her holding him like that . . . He pressed his hand deeper into her jeans and found the soft flesh, then ran his fingertips lightly over her folds. He pushed between them until he found her opening. Then he glided inside. Fuck, the feel of her hot slickness enveloping his fingers drove him wild.

He wrapped his other hand around hers, squeezing him, then guided her hand up and down. She followed his lead, stroking him as he swirled his fingers in her melting heat. He slid out and stroked her slit, then found her clitoris.

She gasped as he stroked it, almost as if she'd never had a man do that to her before.

He wanted to see her, so he grasped her jeans and pulled them down. Her hand fell away from his cock as he moved to pull them off her legs, and then he reached for her panties. He noticed she was biting her lip. He smiled and swooped down for a kiss, then tugged her black panties down her legs. She kicked them away as he gazed at her.

He was right, her pussy was not shaven. He ran his fingers over the curls. So soft and dark. A perfect contrast to her pink petals.

"Do I look strange?" she asked, concern etching her eyes.

"Strange?" He could barely tear his gaze from her lovely pussy to stare at her in a daze.

"Well, I know most girls . . ." She sucked in a breath. "I mean, I didn't know we were going to . . ."

He laughed. "It's fine. It's . . . different."

Disappointment filled her eyes and he realized that— at least in this—she didn't want to be different.

He leaned in and kissed her. "You're perfect," he murmured.

He felt her fingers wrap around his cock again and she stroked.

"Do you want me to go down on you?" she asked uncertainly.

He chuckled. "That would be very nice, but how about I go down on you instead?"

He slid off the couch to his knees, missing the feel of her hand around him as it slipped away. He leaned forward and nuzzled her stomach, then kissed downward to her curls. He stroked over them with both hands, then opened the petals of flesh and licked her.

"Ohhh," she cried.

The sound excited him, and sent his cock lurching. He found her clit and circled it with his tongue, then lapped at it.

"Oh, God," she whimpered, her head lolling back on the couch.

Fuck, she was so responsive.

He suckled and she arched. His hand glided up her side, and then he cupped her breast. She rested her hand on his and squeezed. He rolled his tongue over her bud, then stroked her slit. He slid his finger inside her, his cock twitching with need. Her opening was so hot and inviting and he could hardly wait to drive his cock deep inside her. He suckled her harder as he slid another finger inside.

At her moan, he wanted to pull his fingers free and press his erection to her. To drive in deep and hard. Fuck, maybe she'd like that. He could take her fast and hard now, then again later. He could take her up on her offer of oral sex to get him ready again right away.

He lifted his head, ready to shift into position, but the sight of her face glowing with pleasure took his breath away. He kept gliding his fingers inside her.

"You like that, sweetheart?"

"Ohhh, yes."

Fuck. He could come on the spot.

He leaned forward and licked her clit, to her moan. Then he settled in and tweaked her nub between his lips. He teased and squeezed, then suckled hard.

"Oh, yes. Oh, God." She arched against him.

She was close. His cock ached as he gazed up at her, her hot flesh in his mouth. She breathed in deep pants, and he could feel it. Her body tensing, then arching up against him as she moaned her release. Her face glowed and the sounds she uttered made his whole body tense with need.

"Oh, Kane. That's . . ." Then she whimpered.

He drove his fingers deeper, thrusting gently. Her moans became louder and then . . . Oh, God, she wailed so loudly he feared the neighbors would call the police.

But screw them. He nearly came at the sound of her reedy cries of pleasure.

Finally, her moans faded and she slumped on the couch. He gave her one last lick then flattened his hands on her belly and rested his chin on them, staring up at her with a smile.

"I think you enjoyed that."

Her eyes turned to him and the look of wonder took his breath away.

"I never imagined . . ." Her words trailed off and she just shook her head.

"You've never had a guy do that to you before?"

She shook her head. He couldn't help smiling, pleased he'd been the first to give her that pleasure.

He took her hand and drew her to her feet, then kissed her. She stroked his cheek and deepened the kiss. Her nipples were hard beads pressing into his chest and his cock twitched with need. He eased back and gazed at her naked body.

"You are beautiful."

She smiled timidly. He took her hand and led her to his bedroom. She sat down on the bed as he stripped off his pants, and then shed his boxers. Her gaze was locked on his cock as he walked toward her. She wrapped her hand around him, a look of awe on her face. He stepped closer as she stroked him, her soft hand gliding his length, starting a slow burn inside him. Then she leaned forward and kissed the tip of him.

Her tongue brushed against him, then she opened and slid her lips around him, taking his cockhead into her mouth. She squeezed, her tongue lapping over his tip. Then she started to suck. Her hand continued moving up and down his shaft.

"Oh, God, baby, I love that, but . . ." He drew her away from him. "I really just want to be inside you right now." He smiled. "But I promise you can do that later."

She gazed up at him, looking a little uncertain, and then she lay back on the bed. She opened her legs in invitation, and the sight of her glistening pink folds—reminding him of how sweet and wet she was—had him prowling over her immediately.

He grasped his rock-hard cock in his hand and dragged the tip over her soft, wet flesh.

"Fuck, you feel so good." He centered his cockhead and pushed in a little.

She stiffened beneath him.

"It's okay, baby. I'll go slow."

She was probably a bit intimidated by his size, since he was bigger than most guys he knew.

He pressed a little deeper, the feel of her warmth around him sending his hormones racing. God, he wanted to be buried deep inside her, but he forced himself to move slowly.

But she was so tight, her passage gripping his cockhead snuggly.

She tensed as he pushed deeper.

"I know I'm big, baby, but just relax."

She nodded, but her eyes were filled with apprehension.

He leaned forward and licked her nipple, then suckled softly. She arched against his mouth and he slid a little deeper into her.

She wrapped her arms around him and pulled him closer.

"God, please push inside me."

He kissed up her chest, then nuzzled her neck. "I want to baby, but I'm trying to go slow for you."

"Screw slow. Please do it now."

At her encouragement, he thrust forward. She cried out and he knew something wasn't right. He lifted his head and gazed at her, seeing a tear streaking down her face.

Chapter Six

"What the hell?" As soon as the thought skittered through Kane's brain, he went into shock. "Are you . . . a virgin?"

"Not now."

"Oh, fuck." He tried to pull away, but she clutched him to her chest.

"You aren't going to stop, are you?" she asked in a panicked voice.

"I wish you'd told me. I could have . . ." He could have what? Been gentler?

No, what he would have done was stopped this whole thing.

"Please don't stop." Her wide eyes beseeched him. "Please don't . . . reject me."

Fuck! He kissed her fiercely, then drew back, his cock sliding along her slick passage. He slowly glided forward again. She was still tense, but he stroked out and in again. Slowly. And again. She started to relax and the apprehension in her eyes turned to desire.

He continued filling her, his cock stroking her deeply. She moaned, clinging to his shoulders. Pleasure vibrated through him and the look of absolute bliss on her face filled him with jubilance. He thrust deeply now, loving her moans of pleasure.

"Oh, Kane, it feels so good. I . . ." She gasped. "Oh, God, I . . ."

Then she moaned, her face glowing in pleasure.

He thrust deep into her body, riding her hard as she gasped and trilled. Heat flooded his groin and he tensed, then groaned as he erupted inside her.

He kept pumping as she rode the wave of pleasure, watching her face in blissful abandon.

She was so beautiful.

Finally they collapsed on the bed together. He rolled to his side and pulled her close, her soft body tight against him.

That had been phenomenal. But, fuck, he couldn't believe he'd just taken her virginity. That had never been part of the plan.

Present

"Things seemed to be going pretty well, until I told her about the partnership. That's when she bolted," Kane explained to Will.

Will picked up his coffee again and leaned back in the leather chair.

"I would imagine. So why don't you think it's over?"

"I told her not to be rash and suggested we meet at Hades tomorrow evening."

Will's eyebrow rose. "Do you think she will?"

Kane shrugged. "She wants this pretty badly. But you're right, that may not be enough. So, I'm going to ask you for a favor."

River picked up the tall cocktail the waitress placed in front of her and sucked on the straw. The frozen mango-berry was sweet and delicious and she knew she had to pace herself or she'd drink the whole thing in five minutes.

"Tell me. Why are we sitting here instead of at Hades where the opportunity of a lifetime is waiting for you?" Tia took a sip of her Mango Tango.

"I don't want to sell my soul for a business opportunity."

"Are you worried because you think he'll expect sex from you?"

River poked her straw up and down in the fruity slush. "I know he will."

Tia grinned. "Is he good-looking?"

"What does that have to do with it?"

"Well . . . He's good-looking. Rich. What's the problem?"

"You think I should prostitute myself to get my business going?"

Tia giggled. "You're being way too serious. You guys dated in college. You were obviously attracted to him.

Now he wants to start it up again. It's not like he's some stranger forcing you into something. It sounds like he seriously wants things to work between you."

River glared at her friend. "How would you know? You weren't there."

Tia shrugged. "The romantic in me, I guess."

River stared at her drink. "You don't know. What happened between us . . ." She shook her head, her cheeks flushing.

"You're right, I don't know. Why don't you tell me?"

River's chest constricted. She didn't want to talk about something so painful.

Tia took River's hand and squeezed it. "I mean it, Riv. Tell me about it. Help me understand."

River compressed her lips, and then sucked in a deep breath. "We were different people. He was the well-dressed, clearly-has-money rich kid who had all the right friends and connections and had his whole future mapped out. I was the mess. Crazy hair. Crazy clothes. Trashy family. Hardly any friends."

Tia grinned. "You still dress a little crazy."

"Crazy's a harsh word," River said defensively.

She actually wore a simple black dress tonight, but she glanced down at the black high heels she wore, a little self-consciously. She'd taken a silver Sharpie and drawn an intricate design on them to give them some pizzazz. And the same on her clutch purse so it would match. She wore a beaded necklace. She'd dyed the beads herself—various shades of blue to green—and woven them together to create a multicolored coil with a teardrop crystal hanging from the end, and a tassel of beads below that.

Tia patted her hand. "You know what I mean. And you know that I love your look. And your nail polish." She lifted River's hand and admired her nails. "I'm loving the turquoise!" She arched an eyebrow. "You know I'm still waiting for my bottle of Tia Wanna polish that you promised me. I mean, it's named after me, so it's really cruel of you to make me wait so long."

River laughed. "I'll be getting my supplies next week and I'll make it for you then. I promise."

Tia Wanna wasn't part of the collections she'd done for the Kickstarter, but was part of the next collection she planned to release.

"Okay." Tia sipped her drink. "Now you were saying . . . He was the rich hottie and you were the crazy girl. Go."

River laughed. "I'd argue the crazy, but with what happened . . ." She shrugged. "He just asked me out one day. Right out of the blue."

"Don't tell me. You'd been mooning over him for months and then suddenly, like in a fairy tale, he asked you to the prom and you were swept away."

"You are a nutcase, you know that? It was during exams and he asked me to study."

"Because you were the smart chick?"

"Am I telling this story or are you just going to make stuff up?"

Tia grinned. "We could do both."

River sighed. When Tia had a couple of drinks, she got playful.

"In fact, he was the smart one," River clarified. "At least in chemistry."

"Yeah, chemistry." Tia winked and nudged River's shoulder.

"Tia, do you want to hear, or not?" But River couldn't help the smile curling her lips.

Tia sipped her drink. "Okay, I'll be good." She rested her chin on her hands and put on her listening face.

"He asked me to study, then after the exam he invited me to a party. I felt really out of place."

"And he dumped you because his friends didn't like you?"

River shot her a glance.

"Sorry." Tia sipped her drink.

"No, actually he introduced me to his best friend, who seemed to like me, and both of them stood up for me when guys were rude to me."

"Awww. He sounds great. What happened after the party?"

"I . . ." River stared at her drink. "I went back to his place. And we . . ." She hesitated, and then shrugged.

"You did it. Then he dumped you the next day?"

"It's not like that. He . . . That time was my first."

"Ohhh. Did he take advantage of you? Was he really bad and made you never want to have sex again?"

"No," River said in exasperation. "He was perfect,

okay? Right from the beginning, he was sensitive and caring. He made me feel wanted. He didn't want to push me into anything. And when he found out I was a virgin . . . well, it was too late then . . . but he was unhappy I hadn't told him." She stared into Tia's wide eyes. "He did everything right. He was perfect."

Tia blinked, looking perplexed. "So what's the problem?"

"The problem is that it was all an act."

They sat in silence for a moment and River realized her hands were clenched tightly in her lap. She relaxed them and took another sip of her almost empty drink.

"Excuse me, ladies?"

River glanced up to see the waitress with a bottle of champagne in her hand.

"A gentleman sent this."

Another waiter placed an ice bucket on a stand beside the table as the waitress popped the cork, then filled two tall flutes and set them on the table.

"We should refuse this," River said.

"Don't be a spoilsport," Tia said.

Then River noticed the waitress had poured a third glass.

"No, wait. There's just the two of us," River protested.

"That one's for me."

She glanced up at Kane's voice. "What are you doing here?"

He sat down in the chair beside her. "When you didn't come to me at Hades, I decided to come to you."

"This is Kane?" Tia asked, a smile creeping across her face.

Kane smiled that charming smile of his and shook Tia's hand. "Pleased to meet you."

"I'm Tia," she said, a bit breathlessly, obviously captivated.

Of course, River couldn't really blame her. He was devastatingly handsome in his dark gray suit, his wavy hair immaculate, his indigo eyes glittering with sincerity. And the delightfully masculine scent of his musky aftershave made a girl feel all feminine and needy.

"How did you know I was here?" River demanded.

"Well, I assumed you might decide not to show up so I had a backup plan."

"And that was to stalk me?"

"Just because I used Will's hacking skills to track your cell phone, doesn't mean I'm a stalker."

"I think that's exactly what it means."

As River glared at him, Tia sipped her champagne, her gaze shifting from River to Kane. Then it held on Kane and her eyes grew dreamy.

"Thank you for the champagne," Tia said. "Are we celebrating something?"

He gazed at River, his eyes searching hers. "I had hoped we'd be celebrating our new partnership."

"I already told you," River said. "It's never going to happen."

"That's unfortunate." He sipped his champagne and settled back in the chair. "So Tia, what do you do?"

River sat watching as Kane chatted with Tia. Asking about her life and interests. Charming her until River thought Tia would swoon. The waitress came by and filled their glasses again, then took away the empty bottle. Kane ordered another round of drinks. Two more Mango Tangos and a scotch—aged a ridiculous number of years—on the rocks for him.

"Kane, I don't mean to be rude," River finally said as Kane sipped his scotch, "but Tia and I were enjoying a girls' night."

"Of course. I'll finish my drink and leave you to it."

"Oh, no," said Tia. "Do you really have to go?"

River sent her a sharp glance and Tia just grinned.

He downed the rest of his drink, then took Tia's hand and kissed it. At the look of enchantment in her eyes, River was afraid Tia would float away on a cloud. Then he leaned toward River and his fingers glided through her hair as he cupped her head, easing her closer. Before she could protest, his lips captured hers. Her body failed her, refusing to pull away when she ordered it to. Then she melted into the kiss. Breathing in his musky aftershave. Luxuriating in the strength of his arms as they slid around her.

The ache became unbearable. A yearning so intense it terrified her.

Then he released her. His knowing eyes searched hers . . . and he smiled.

He reached into his pocket and pulled out a business card and pressed it into her hand.

"Call me if you change your mind."

"I won't." She tossed the card on the table.

The confidence shining in his eyes didn't waver.

He turned to Tia. "It was nice meeting you, Tia."

"The pleasure was all mine," Tia said with a wide smile.

He turned and walked away.

"Tia, stop staring at his butt."

Tia giggled. "Why? It's such a fine butt." She shook her head. "I don't know what he did after popping your cherry, but hon, you are crazy not to take him up on his offer." She watched Kane disappear around the corner. "A man like that is hard to find."

River sighed. "Is that all we're going to talk about now?"

"No, of course not." Tia picked up the discarded business card and slipped it into her purse.

River chose to say nothing about it. They enjoyed the rest of the evening without another word about Kane . . . until they asked for the bill. Kane had arranged to pay for the whole thing. And when they stepped outside, there was a limo waiting to take them home.

"No way," River said. "We can take the bus."

"But it's raining," Tia complained, taking River's arm. "And I've never been inside a limo. Come on. For me?"

River relented and climbed into the car with Tia, half fearing Kane would be inside.

He wasn't.

River settled into the soft, supple leather seat. She could imagine Kane sitting beside her, totally at home in the luxurious vehicle.

The driver dropped Tia off first, and then pulled up in front of River's apartment building. He opened the car door for her, then rushed ahead to open the glass door to the building.

"Thank you," she said as she stepped inside.

When she reached her apartment, she kicked off her shoes and slumped down on the couch.

If only Tia had understood. After Kane had "popped her cherry," as Tia had put it, he'd then stolen something much more valuable from her.

First year of college—Spring semester

River opened her eyes to the soft sunlight glowing through the drawn curtains. Kane was behind her, his arms around her, holding her snug to his body from head to toe.

Oh, God, that had been the most incredible experience of her life. Kane had made her ascension into womanhood a wonderful, life-changing event.

She turned in his arms and rested her head against his chest, listening to his rhythmic heartbeat. He stroked her hair from her face, his fingers brushing lightly across her cheek then over her temple. Her skin tingled at his touch.

She gazed up at him and smiled timidly, suddenly feeling shy. "You're awake."

His expression was somber. Her chest constricted.

"What's wrong, Kane?" Had she done something to upset him?

"Last night . . . I wish you'd told me."

She leaned her face against his chest again. "It's not important."

He rolled her onto her back and pinned her with his gaze.

"Why didn't you tell me?"

His tone wasn't accusing. In fact, the way he looked at her—his eyes filled with concern—made her feel protected and cared for.

"I didn't want you to think I was a freak."

His expression turned puzzled.

"Why would I think that?"

"Have you met any girls here who are still virgins?"

He grinned. "Well, I haven't done a poll . . ."

She laughed. "No, but you've probably been with half the freshman girls, so you've seen a pretty big sample."

His eyebrow arched. "Are you calling me a slut?"

"No, you're a guy. Everyone just considers you a ladies' man. If I'd slept with as many guys, then I'd be considered a slut. The unfair double standard."

He leaned in close and kissed her, his lips lingering on hers, then brushing across her cheek, sending tingles dancing through her.

"River, I would never think you're a freak. And I want you to know that last night was special for me, too."

She wrapped her arms around his neck and pulled him back for another kiss. She pressed her tongue between his lips and swept inside. His tongue met hers and they tangled, then he suckled. Her pulse quickened and she took his hand and drew it to her naked breast.

"Last night was so great," she said breathlessly. "And I think it'll only get better with practice."

He squeezed her breast. Her nipple hardened, and she ached to feel his mouth around it. She dragged her palm down his chest, over his sculpted abs, and then her fingers brushed lightly over his cock. It wasn't as big as last night, or as hard, but as she wrapped her hand around it, it swelled.

"I love how enthusiastic you are."

"Yeah?" She stroked his hardening cock. "Well, I want to make up for lost time. You're such a great tutor . . ." She squeezed his erection, loving how hard it was, then stroked up and down. "I'm hoping you'll teach me some new things."

He groaned. "Sweetheart, right now you're doing just fine."

She watched his face as her hand glided up and down his thick shaft. She loved how the skin, which was as soft as kid leather, moved over the iron-hard column beneath. And the look of growing pleasure on his face enthralled her.

She continued stroking him, watching his rapt expression. She pressed her hand against his chest and pushed him until he rolled onto his back, then she knelt between his knees. She leaned forward and pressed her lips to the tip of his cock—her hand still moving—and kissed it. His eyes grew needier as he watched her.

God, she felt so powerful being able to affect him like this.

"I didn't really get a good look at this last night." She stopped pumping and stared at his cock. It stood straight up, like a skyscraper reaching for the stars.

She'd never really seen a penis, but she was sure this one was a masterpiece. Of course, her opinion was colored by the vast amount of pleasure it had given her last night.

The head, which was as big as a clementine, was purple-red and mushroom-shaped, and veins pulsed along the thick shaft. She ran her finger from the base of the solid column to the tip.

"You're right. You are big."

"How do you know? It's not like you have anything to compare it to."

"Maybe not, but my roommate likes to talk about sex. A *lot*."

"And she talks about how big guys are?"

She nodded. "And what she does with them and how good they are. And she gives me tips."

"Yeah? What kind of tips?"

She grinned. "Like this."

Chapter Seven

River grasped his cock and pressed her lips to the tip, then opened to take the head inside. It filled her mouth. She pumped him slowly as she ran her tongue around the top, then over the small opening, tasting the salty drop oozing from it.

She watched his face, seeing how much what she was doing was pleasing him. She sucked, squeezing him inside her mouth. Watching his pleasure grow. Then she swallowed, causing a deeper suction. To her satisfaction, he groaned. His fingers glided through her hair and he cupped her head, then drew her forward. She took him deeper. Gloria had told her when giving a guy head, especially a big guy, to tip her head back and relax the throat so she could take him deeper.

She'd always been a bit uncomfortable with Gloria's obsession over talking about sex, but at the intense need in Kane's eyes, she was so glad she'd listened.

She took him as deep as she could, then slid back, her hand following, then eased deep again.

"Oh, fuck, that is so good."

She moved faster on him, loving the feel of his rigid flesh gliding past her lips. Loving the musky masculine scent of him and his soft groans of pleasure.

"I'm going to come soon, sweetheart," he warned.

His hand urged her head to move faster.

"Fuck, baby, you need to pull off now."

But she wanted to continue bringing him pleasure. To ride all the way to the edge with him, squeezing him between her lips. He groaned and hot, salty liquid filled her mouth. She kept pumping him as she swallowed all of it.

When he was finished, she licked him, and then slid up beside him on the bed, a smile on her face. His arm was tossed over his face and he was sucking in air. She stroked his chest.

"You liked that?" she asked.

A rumble started in his chest and suddenly, she found herself rolled back and he was over her, his arms on either side of her head as he stared down at her.

"Fuck yeah." Then his lips consumed hers, his tongue driving into her mouth.

His hand cupped her breast and she arched against him, wanting to feel his hands all over her. His lips slid to her neck and he nuzzled, sending tingles dancing along her spine.

"Tell your roommate thanks for me," he rumbled.

She giggled, hormones and adrenaline creating a heady rush of exhilaration.

He kissed down her chest then gazed at her breasts in awe, making her cheeks flush. Then he captured her nipple in his mouth and it was her turn to groan. He lapped at her sensitive flesh, and then suckled.

"Ohhh, yes."

He moved to the other nipple and lapped at the pebbled aureole, then sucked. She raked her nails over his back, pulling him tighter to her.

Then she felt it. His heavy cock, swollen to solid rock again, resting on her belly. He grasped it and pressed it to her folds. She could feel the slickness as he glided the tip along her slit.

"I want to fuck you again." He kept gliding over her wet flesh, waiting for her approval.

"I want you to."

He smiled, then pressed his cockhead against her. Slowly, it pushed into her, stretching her. The whole cockhead slid inside, feeling massive inside her tender passage. She was still sore from their first session, yet she welcomed the sweet pleasure-pain of him inside her.

She watched him, her eyes wide with wonder.

"You okay?" he asked.

She nodded, opening her legs wider. He slid his arms under her knees and tucked them over his shoulders, widening her even more. Then he eased deeper.

He was so thick and hard. He inched deeper still, her vagina clutching him tightly. When he was only partway in, he reversed direction, his cockhead dragging back along her passage. Then he pushed forward, going deeper again.

Each time he pulled back, he followed with a deeper thrust. Each stroke of his cock sent quivers through her, pleasure coiling deep inside. When he finally pushed all the way in, he stopped and kissed her. She tightened her arms around him and kissed him back with passionate abandon.

Oh, God, she wanted to be like this forever. Him deep inside her, giving her pleasure. Her giving him pleasure.

He started to move, his cock gliding inside her, driving her pleasure higher. His thick, hard shaft stroked her and she squeezed, heightening the sensations.

"Fuck, baby, yeah." He nuzzled her neck as he thrust.

She felt it blossom inside her. Deeper and more intense than last night. Swirling through her. Building like a giant tornado. An orgasm of epic proportions. Her whole body began to tremble and she clung to him, her senses ablaze.

"Oh, God. . . ." She gasped as bliss swelled through her. She hung on to him. Tight. "Kane, oh . . . yes . . ." Then a wail tore from her throat as her whole world exploded. Blasting into a million pieces as she shattered around him.

He groaned and thrust deep, pinning her to the bed. Liquid heat filled her and she clutched him tight as they both shuddered in release.

Then they just lay there, holding each other.

A glowing warmth filled her. She never wanted to let him go. She wanted to be his forever.

Warning bells blared inside her head, telling her it was too much, too soon. That she couldn't expect any of that, but she ignored them. She couldn't help herself. Everything inside her told her he was the man she was meant to be with. The man she wanted to spend her life with.

And he clearly wanted her, too.

She knew somehow she would find a way to make it work.

River spent the morning with Kane. They played some pool in the game room in his building, then went back to his apartment and enjoyed some more intimate time together. She fell asleep, then woke up to find he'd made lunch.

She sat down at the table, then took a bite of the spaghetti with meat sauce he'd set in front of her.

"So what's your family like?" she asked.

He handed her a glass of soda, then sat across from her.

"It's just me and my parents. My dad is a serious type, a bit crusty, but really smart. And he's very strong willed. Mom is kind of sweet. She softens his rough edges."

She liked the warmth in his eyes as he talked about them.

"Dad's more or less retired now," Kane continued. "He used to work long hours, seven days a week, and Mom and I used to worry about him. Then a couple of years ago, he had a heart attack and then . . . bang! . . . in his usual sure-minded way, he decided life was too short and put his company in the hands of his well-trained executives. Now he oversees any major undertakings, but mostly he and Mom spend a lot of time together traveling." He smiled, his eyes lighting up. "They're so much happier since he made that decision."

"Where are they now?" she asked.

"They've gone to Paris for a few months. In the fall, they might go back to New York for a while before they jet off to somewhere warm for the winter."

"With all that traveling, do you get to see them much?" she asked.

He seemed so close to his parents. With them away all the time, he must miss them.

"I visit them every few months, when school permits. And we keep in touch over Skype."

She frowned. "It sounds a bit lonely for you."

He sipped his soda. "I'm fine. I have a lot of friends and . . ." He shrugged. "I like my independence."

He gazed at her and smiled. "I can tell you think I feel abandoned, but I don't. I know if I asked them to spend more time nearby, they would. But we don't have to be in the same city . . . or even country . . . to be close. I know they love me. They've shown me that in everything they've said and done for me my whole life."

She gazed at him with new eyes. She had thought he was a spoiled rich kid, with no appreciation of what his family gave him. That his relationship with his family would be superficial and distant.

But what he had was something she craved. Parents who cared about her and her well-being. Who would be willing to put aside their own wants, if only for a moment, to look out for her and ensure she was okay.

Parents who loved her.

After lunch, he drove her to the small house where she rented a room in the basement and walked her to the back door, then gave her a passionate kiss. She walked inside, a big smile on her face, then opened the door to the stairs and went down to the small apartment she shared with Gloria. Gloria had been a stranger to River when they both moved in in September—both just students the homeowners had rented rooms to. They hadn't become close friends, and at one time River wished Gloria hadn't been such an over-sharer about her sex life, though now she was grateful for it.

When she reached the bottom of the stairs, she saw Gloria sitting on the couch reading a book.

"Hi, Gloria."

Gloria put down her book and stared at her. River could sense the tension emanating from her.

"You spent the night with Kane Winters?"

"Uh . . . yeah. Why?"

Gloria stood up. "I hate to be the one to tell you this," she said tightly. "But . . . he was only using you."

"What are you talking about?"

Gloria shrugged. "He's a guy and that's what they do."

Anger surged through River and she planted her hands on her hips. "Is it that hard to believe he's actually interested in me?"

"Because he was sweet and charming and told you what you wanted to hear?" she challenged. "River, that's what guys do to get into a girl's pants. Plus . . . he only went out with you on a bet."

River blinked as those last words sank in. Then her blood slowly turned to ice.

"No, I don't believe that." But her stomach clenched, uncertainty seeping through her.

"He just wanted to nail you, River."

Gloria picked up her phone from the crate that acted as a coffee table. "Listen."

She pushed a button, and the sounds of moaning emanated from the phone.

"Oh, God!"

"You like that, sweetheart." It was Kane's voice.

"Ohhh, yes." . . . moaning . . . *"Oh, yes. Oh, God."*

River's cheeks flushed hotly

"Oh, Kane. That's . . ." Then there was a whimpering sound.

River stared at Gloria in horror. "Where did you get that?"

"Several friends e-mailed it to me."

"Oh, God." River felt as if she was going to be sick.

The recording—which had clearly been edited to showcase the highlights of her humiliation—went on, but at some point, all River could hear was the sound of blood rushing to her ears. She felt like she might pass out.

"There's a part where you tell him you learned your awesome blow job skills from your roommate, who's been

with a lot of guys." Gloria flicked off the phone, glaring
at her. "Thanks a lot for dragging my name into the mud
with yours. If you come back in the fall, do me a favor
and get another roommate."

Gloria stomped off to her room and all River could
do was sink onto the couch in total shock. If she didn't
come back here in the fall, she'd lose her scholarship but . . .
how could she possibly come back?

Her heart ached. But worse, how could she possibly
be on the same campus as Kane Winters after he'd de-
ceived her and then betrayed her so cruelly?

Present

River stashed her purse in her locker, and stared at her reflection in the mirror on the locker door. God, she looked
like crap. She hadn't slept well.

She sighed, knowing she might as well get used to
that with having to work in the evenings to get her new
business off the ground. But last night, she'd been reliv-
ing the memory of Kane's betrayal. And grieving the fact
that she'd had to turn down the opportunity to have her
nail polish carried in such a prestigious boutique as Rapture. That would have made her brand elite and in high
demand.

Actually, getting into any store would be fabulous.
Most indie brands she knew of sold online.

But she couldn't become partners with Kane. Not after
what he'd done.

She walked onto the floor and said hi to the other girls

working today. The pace was steady during her shift, and slowed late in the afternoon.

As River finished with a customer, Louise walked over to her.

"River, come into the office," she said.

River followed her through the door at the back of the store and into the office. Louise sat down at the desk.

"I'm sorry but I'm going to have to let you go."

"What?" River stared at her, her stomach clenching. "I don't understand."

"You've received a couple of warnings."

"About the nail polish I wear?" She glanced at her nails. She'd used Seafoam today. Nothing fancy, just three coats—no extra design—and a top coat. No chips.

"Not just that. You haven't been supportive of the store programs and don't even seem to try. And, quite frankly, I know you're starting your own business and I really want people working here who are serious about staying. There are lots of people looking for a job who will be happy to work here and gladly follow the rules."

River did her best to tamp down the anger surging through her. "Louise, I am supportive of the store's programs and I'll do better."

"I'm sorry. Today is your last day. I've already scheduled people into your shifts."

River just stared at her in shock.

"Your shift is over," Louise said, her gaze cold, "so get your stuff from your locker and go."

·   ·   ·

"Oh, God, I don't know what to do." River stared at Tia across the table in the coffee shop.

"You have that money from your Kickstarter campaign. Can't you use that to live on until you get a new job?"

"No, I've already spent it on the business."

She had hoped to secure a lot of new clients from the people who'd donated to Kickstarter, but all the bottles of polish were going to Kane. She'd used all the profits to buy enough materials to make even more polish to put up for sale and she planned to send a lot out to beauty bloggers and YouTube stars who did fashion and makeup tutorials in hopes they'd talk up her brand.

"Also, I've spent some money on a Web site design so I can start selling online."

She'd also paid for ads on some high-traffic blogs. It all cost money and she'd seriously dipped into her savings, too.

"So you'll start bringing money in soon," Tia said hopefully.

"Not enough to live on. And it'll take time to build sales . . . if I get any at all."

Tia patted her hand. "Don't think like that. You're going to do great. I know you are."

"But what do I live on until then?"

"Well . . . you know you could always reconsider . . ."

"No. Don't even say it." River sipped her coffee, but it tasted sour in her mouth.

"I know you really don't want to, but you're only hurting yourself." Tia opened her purse and pulled out Kane's business card. She handed it to River. "Call him."

Chapter Eight

River shook her head.

"Look, whatever he did," Tia said, "he seems to want to make up for it. And even if you won't forgive him, there's no reason you shouldn't take what he has to offer. Just tell him it's business only and that's it."

"He wants to be my partner."

"So set out guidelines being clear that you're in charge."

River pursed her lips, staring at Kane's card.

"Don't shoot yourself in the foot, Riv. This is the opportunity of a lifetime. Don't let what he did to you in the past control your future."

River stared at the card sitting on her desk. Kane's card.

Don't let what he did to you in the past control your future.

Tia was right.

River was being stubborn because she felt taking anything from Kane would make him think he'd made up

for what he'd done to her. He could never make it up . . .
and her pain would never go away completely . . . but she
had to move forward. Thinking that she was causing him
pain because she wouldn't let him help her was naïve on
her part. He would probably just shrug it off, perfectly
happy with the thought that he'd done his best. She was
stupid to think he'd lose even one night's sleep over it if
she shunned his deal.

Yet she had so much to lose. This was her dream.

She picked up the phone.

Kane glanced at the display on his ringing cell phone and
smiled.

"Hello, River."

"Hi. I . . . uh . . . wanted to thank you for paying for
our drinks the other day."

"Really? I thought you might resent that."

And he wished she didn't. He wanted to do things for
her. He wished he could do more, but didn't want to over-
whelm her.

"But you did it anyway."

"Well, it seems I was wrong." But he knew he wasn't
and that she was just making polite conversation. Something must have changed and she was reconsidering his
offer.

"It was nice of you."

He was sure she was gritting her teeth while saying it,
even though her words sounded sincere.

"And the limo? When I saw it had started to rain, I

thought you might particularly appreciate not taking the bus."

"Yes, Tia had never been in a limo before. She was very impressed."

"And what about you, River?"

"I'd never been in a limo before either."

He smiled at her refusal to give an inch, even while wishing she actually appreciated his gesture.

"So why are you calling?"

She sighed. "I want to know if . . . Could we meet again?"

"You're asking me out on a date?"

"No," she said sharply. "I mean . . . uh . . . I want to know if it's too late to take you up on your offer. Of getting my nail polish into Rapture."

"I'm willing to meet and talk about that. I have some time tomorrow. I'll send a car for you at five p.m.

"At five?"

"Do you have a problem with the time?"

"No. I'll be waiting."

His first inclination had been to suggest she meet with him this evening. He already had the contract drawn up and it sounded like she was anxious to talk to him. But since she'd made it clear she wasn't going to give them another chance romantically, he had to do something to convince her otherwise. An idea he'd been toying with suddenly seemed the only solution, so he would make a quick call to his lawyer to have some modifications made. He intended to ensure she had little choice in the matter.

．   ．   ．

River paced the pavement in front of the entrance to her apartment building. She hated this. Kane sending a car and setting meeting times. But what she hated most was how much she needed his help.

She'd be damned if she'd have some chauffeur summoning her down when he arrived, so she decided to wait outside.

It was getting a little cool, so she pulled on her blazer and glanced at her reflection in the glass as she drew her long dark hair over the collar and smoothed it down. She wore a nice shirt with a pair of new jeans. She'd debated whether to wear a skirt for the meeting, but decided casual was a better approach. The shirt and blazer were a nod to the business nature of their meeting, and the jeans said she wasn't stressing about the outcome. Now if only she could get her face and demeanor on board.

A shiny black car pulled up in front of her building. Not an elegant limo like the other night, but a town car.

Was he being sensitive to her discomfort at lavish luxury?

No, he probably just didn't want to spend the money. She'd already shown him she would not be impressed by his wealth.

She sighed. Even though she was going to gain from it by partnering with him.

The driver opened the door and she slid inside.

She was surprised when the driver took the parkway

by the canal instead of heading to the market area where the trendy bars were, including Hades.

"Excuse me. Where are we going?" she asked the driver.

He glanced at her in the rearview mirror. "We're going to Mr. Winters's residence, ma'am."

Her stomach clenched. She was going to his apartment?

They drove through a residential area with elegant homes behind wrought-iron fences. The driver turned into a driveway and the gate opened, then he drove up the curved path to a large, stately home.

There was a lovely garden out front with peach tulips and purple hyacinths in bloom. There were wide steps up to the elegant double doors with stained-glass windows.

He opened her door and walked with her to the entrance.

"Mr. Winters said to go right in and sit down." He opened the door for her.

She stepped into the house and her eyes widened at the luxurious surroundings. The foyer had cream marble floors and a curved staircase leading to a second level. A chandelier with glittering crystals hung from the ceiling.

She glanced around and saw a living room on her right, glass French doors on her left, and a hallway beside the staircase leading to other rooms. She wasn't sure which direction to go. He'd said to come in and sit down. She noticed a settee in the foyer, so she sat down there.

As she waited nervously, she realized she was way out of her depth. Not only was she intimidated by this lavish house, she was going to partner with a man who ran a huge corporation. She was well aware of how successful Synergetic—the company Kane had started with Will—had become. It was leading the edge in many new technologies and had become almost a household name.

And yet he was partnering with her for a small nail polish company.

To assuage his guilt. And to encourage her to continue their relationship—which meant he wanted sex—but that was not going to happen.

"There you are. Why are you sitting out here?" Kane stood in the entrance to the living room, looking way too handsome in a pair of designer jeans and casual blue shirt with a thin red stripe.

"The driver said to sit and wait."

"I assumed you'd go into the living room and make yourself comfortable."

Was he kidding? There was nothing about this situation that made her comfortable.

She stood up and followed him into the large room, which was filled with an eclectic mix of furniture in tasteful neutral tones. She sat down on the couch and he sat beside her.

Far too close for her comfort.

He poured a glass of wine from a full bottle on the coffee table and handed it to her.

"You have a nice home," she said, then sipped the wine.

"Thanks. I have an apartment right downtown, but I often spend weekends here. It's quiet, and a great place to entertain."

She couldn't imagine having more than one place to live. And such a big place for only one person. His apartment was probably a huge penthouse, too.

"So you've changed your mind about my offer?"

She put down her wineglass and sat up straighter. "Yes. Well, I thought we could discuss it."

"What happened?"

Her gaze darted to his. "Why do you think—?"

"You were adamant against the idea last time we talked, so I'm just curious what changed your mind."

She was sure telling him put her in a worse negotiating situation but . . . she couldn't lie.

"I lost my job. So I thought rather than working for someone else, I should invest that time in my future."

Also, before finding the job at Giselle's, she'd been unemployed for over a year and she just couldn't handle that again. She had to make this company work.

"Good. I figured that's what you wanted to talk about so I went to the liberty of bringing the partnership papers. We just have to sign."

"Oh . . . I . . . thought we'd just be talking about it today. I didn't realize you'd have me signing something."

"No point in waiting."

"Okay, but . . ." She drew in a breath as she drew her shoulders back. "We need to discuss some terms."

"You're right, we do."

She stood up, thrown off by his relaxed demeanor. She started to pace.

"I want us to be very clear on one thing. This is a business arrangement only," she said. "There will be no personal involvement between us at all. Business meetings only." She glanced around. "And preferably in an office or somewhere over coffee."

"Absolutely not."

She spun around to face him. "What?"

"I don't agree to that at all." He stood up and walked toward her. She had to stop herself from backing up.

"River, I told you . . ." He stood close to her now. "I want to explore what we had." His finger brushed her cheek, and he swept her hair behind her ear, sending tingles along her neck. "I want to kiss you. To touch you." He smiled. "I want to see where this relationship might have gone."

"It wouldn't have gone anywhere," she said through gritted teeth.

His smile grew wider. "You see, that's where I think you're wrong." His fingers slid behind her neck and he drew her forward, then his lips brushed hers.

Nooo, she didn't want to . . .

Her heart beat frantically as his lips moved on hers and, heaven help her, she couldn't stop herself from responding. His other hand slid to her waist and drew her closer as his tongue slid into her mouth.

She could barely breathe. She could barely think.

All she wanted was to melt against him. To succumb to the intense desire thrumming through her. To give herself over to him completely.

His lips drew away and he gazed down at her with smug satisfaction.

"You see, the chemistry has always been great between us. And I think we'd both like to see where it might lead."

"So you want to have sex with me as part of the deal?"

"No. I want to have sex with you because we both want it. I'm quite happy to admit that what I shared with you physically was the best sex I've ever had."

She pulled away from him, her cheeks flushing.

"Is that why you recorded it and spread it all over school?"

She turned her back to him and walked toward the window, needing space.

He frowned. "I'm sorry, River. I didn't mean to remind you . . ." He sighed. "I think it's time I explain. I was never involved in that. I knew you wouldn't believe me, so I wanted to give you time to get to know me . . . to understand that I would never do something like that."

"So you're saying you didn't go out with me on a bet?" The words burned from her mouth like acid pellets.

"I did. But when I met you . . . when we talked . . . we hit it off."

"And then you nailed me."

"That was never part of the bet."

"So you say."

"And why would I lie?"

She placed her hands on her hips. "Everything that happened between us was a lie."

He grasped her shoulder and turned her around, and then she was in his arms, his mouth on hers. His tongue drove into her. His arms tightened around her. His body so close . . . the musky scent of his aftershave . . . his lips moving on hers . . . overwhelmed her senses.

Memories of their bodies entwined so long ago rampaged through her.

She wanted him. God help her. She wanted to be naked in his arms. Feeling his thick cock gliding inside her.

He released her lips, his indigo eyes locked on hers. "This wasn't a lie. The way we are together. The way we make each other feel."

She shook her head. "What you did . . ." Tears welled in her eyes at the remembered humiliation of hearing that recording. And worse . . . the intense sense of betrayal. She pulled from his arms and backed away. "I couldn't go back in the fall. I dropped out."

"You dropped out of college because of me?"

"My scholarship wasn't transferable and I didn't have money like you did."

"I'm sorry, River. I didn't know."

"Now you do."

His lips compressed. "Look, I've always wanted to explain about the recording. At the time, I didn't know how it happened. I swear I didn't make it."

"Are you saying your apartment was bugged?" She didn't believe him for a minute.

"In a way. It was a practical joke. The guys I hung out with got someone to hack my phone to act like a listening device. They activated it before the party. They heard everything within range of my phone the whole time. I didn't know anything about it."

"You didn't know about the recording?"

"Not until someone e-mailed it to me. At first I thought maybe you had . . . but as I listened to it, I realized you would never . . . I was just as much a victim as you were."

She glared at him. "A recording like that would only serve to up your reputation. But for me it was humiliating."

His eyes filled with sympathy and he stepped toward her, but she dodged sideways.

"No matter what the truth is about the recording, you still led me on so you could get into my pants."

"No. It's true I first asked you out on a bet, but everything that happened after that was because I really liked you."

She crossed her arms. "This isn't getting us anywhere. I thought we were here to talk business."

"Of course." He gestured toward the couch and she went and sat down again.

He picked up his briefcase, which was sitting beside the couch, and opened it, then brought out a folder and set it on the coffee table. He opened it and handed her a sheaf of papers held together with a paper clip.

"This agreement details what we've already discussed. The part about the deal with Rapture is written in there, too."

She nodded, relieved he'd done that.

"What about control of the company?" Her stomach tightened, worried he would insist on control.

"It's your idea and your company so you should maintain full control."

Her gaze darted to his. "Really?"

"Of course."

She smiled, surprised at his generosity.

"But since I'll be the sole investor, there is something I ask in return."

She kept her expression calm. She was quite sure she knew what he wanted in return.

"Turn to the last page of the agreement," he said.

He'd put sexual terms in the contract? She flipped to the last page and skimmed the neatly laid out paragraphs. Then froze two-thirds down the page. Her eyes widened.

"You want me to marry you?"

Chapter Nine

"Don't look so shocked. It's a marriage of convenience."

"What's convenient about it?" River demanded.

He shrugged. "It just makes things easier. I want regular sex. As I said, sex with you is the best I've ever had, so why not?"

"What about love?"

"Overrated. Look, I'm a busy guy. Wooing women, dating, all the games . . . it's time-consuming. Having a regular partner will just make it easier. For both of us."

She assumed he worried about things like propriety and social expectations, so screwing around with a lot of women might not be how he wanted people to see him. Being married, with a wife by his side at social functions . . . that's probably how he wanted to portray himself.

"Remember, you're starting a new business. That means lots of hours. There'll be no time to meet guys. Plus, if you're my wife, you don't have to worry about being profitable right away. All your needs will be covered."

"Because I'll be living with you." She was numb. The whole idea was insane.

"Marriage doesn't have to be about love. It can be a practical arrangement that benefits both parties."

"Oh, stop," she said dryly. "You're sweeping me off my feet."

He smiled. "Would you like flowers and candlelight? And me on bended knee?"

"Of course not." Because that would be a lie just like in college. At least now he was being honest. "You can't seriously think—"

"But I do. I know how much you want this deal. And you already know how great we are together physically. This is a great arrangement for you because you have full security. As the contract says, as long as we're married, you fully control the company, so you can do whatever you want with it. And you don't have to worry about money, so you can just concentrate on following your dream."

Her jaw was clenched so tight her throat hurt. She wanted this opportunity. More than anything.

But to marry Kane to get it?

The irony was, after those two short days with him in college, she was sure she'd been falling in love with him.

The fact that he wanted to help her with her company showed her that he really did want to make up for what happened. The fact he still cared—or even remembered—after all this time meant he really must have felt guilty. And maybe it was true that he'd had nothing to do with the recording.

But that didn't mean she should marry him.

He'd said she was the best sex he'd ever had and a part of her was delighted about that.

So all the sex she wanted with a guy who was amazing and sensitive in bed and she would have no financial worries as she built her business.

"I'd like to talk this over with my girlfriend."

"No. I want to be absolutely clear about this. I don't want you to tell anyone about this. As far as everyone knows, this will be a real marriage. I proposed and you accepted."

"I can't tell Tia?"

"The only people who will know are you, me, Will, and the lawyer who drew up the contract."

"How soon do I need to decide?"

"I have my jet standing by to take us to Vegas and a suite is already booked."

"Now? But—"

"Once a decision's been made, I don't believe in waiting."

"But I haven't decided."

"What do you have to lose? If you find you don't like the situation, you can always divorce me."

"Again, you certainly have a way of turning a girl's head." She paced. "Going into a marriage with the idea of divorce as a likely outcome just seems wrong."

Kane walked in front of her, stopping her pacing, then wrapped his hands around her forearms. Heat skittered through her.

"I'm hoping that's not how this will end. I really am in this for the long run. I think it's an ideal arrangement that will work beautifully if we both really try and make it work."

"Why do you think it will work?"

He shrugged. "A lot of cultures have arranged marriages and they work. Why can't this? Especially if we're motivated."

"Like making it a clause that I lose control of my company if I divorce you?"

"If you don't agree to it, you won't even have a company."

His words hit home. Hard. He was right. Looking for a new job would take all her time and energy, and leave her stressed. She wouldn't have the emotional resources left to work on building her business, let alone money for the physical resources.

She sighed.

She wasn't willing to give up her dream.

Could she really marry this totally sexy, gorgeous guy who was great in bed . . . who had broken her heart?

She stuck out her hand. "Okay. It's a deal."

River had never been on a private jet before and it was hard to hide how impressed she was at the luxurious leather seats and the high-quality service of the staff who brought them drinks and a lavish meal, including an entrée of lobster pasta that was better than anything she'd ever tasted.

When they got off the plane, a limo took them to a lovely chapel. Not like the neon-signed, tacky ones she'd seen in sitcoms and movies. It was a charming stone building with stained-glass windows and a heavy oak door with intricate designs carved in the thick wooden door frame.

The driver opened the car door. Kane got out, and offered his hand to her. She took it as he helped her out of the limo, and he continued to hold it as they walked up the stone steps to the chapel door.

They stepped into an entryway with wooden paneling and stairs leading up. As they walked up the stairs, her nervousness increased.

Kane glanced at her. "Your hand is shaking. Are you nervous?"

"I'm about to get married. Of course I'm nervous."

He squeezed her hand and, even though he was the cause of her anxiety, it was somehow reassuring.

"I have a surprise for you."

They reached the top of the stairs and she gazed at him.

"You mean something more surprising than the fact I'm getting married right now?"

He chuckled. "No, I suppose not, but I hope you'll like it."

An older woman with a big smile and welcoming blue eyes greeted them and led them into a room with a sofa and armchairs.

"When you're ready, let me know and we'll start the

service," she said, then slipped from the room, closing the door behind her.

On the sofa was a large, flat box—maroon with a huge white bow.

River walked to the sofa. "Is this the surprise?"

He laughed. "You're very perceptive," he teased.

She just shook her head. "But I have nothing for you."

His indigo eyes glittered. "Well, that's not really true."

Then her cheeks flushed. She quickly turned to the box and lifted the lid. Inside, nestled in maroon tissue paper, was a white satin gown. She picked it up and drew it from the box. It was a strapless sheath that flared below the knees. The bodice was edged with lace, sequins, and pearls. In the box, there was also a beautiful headpiece of lace and satin flowers with two short tufts of fine tulle spraying from each side.

"It's . . . beautiful."

"I didn't think you'd want to get married in your jeans."

Her heart fluttered. This whole thing was crazy, but River was a firm believer in taking big, wild chances. And right now, the man standing in front of her was a chance she knew she had to take.

"There should be shoes in there, too," he said. "And stockings."

She noticed a shoe box tucked in the corner of the larger box, partially hidden by the tissue paper. She opened the box and drew in a breath. Inside were white satin shoes with high, narrow heels, edged with lace, sequins, and pearls, just like the dress. They were elegant and sexy. There was also a pair of long white gloves.

"I'm going to leave you to change. When you're ready, text me."

She watched his retreating back. "Kane," she said as he reached the door.

He turned. "Yes?"

She smiled tremulously. "Thank you."

He sent her a broad smile, and then left the room.

She walked to the door and turned the lock. She noticed a full-length mirror on one wall and an open door to a bathroom. She freshened up, brushing her hair and fixing her makeup. She glanced at her nails. Today, she was wearing a sunset gradient, from deep mauve shifting subtly through pink to orange to yellow on the tips. Not exactly a wedding mani. Good thing there were gloves.

She found the stockings he'd mentioned in the bag, along with a lacy white garter belt and a white satin evening bag. She changed, then sat and put on the shoes. She went into the bathroom and grabbed an elastic and some hair pins from her purse and swept her hair up into a ponytail, then took one tress and wrapped it around the elastic to cover it. She set the headpiece on her head, pulling her hair up through the opening. She spread the tufts of tulle wider until it formed a halo around her head.

As she pulled on the gloves, she realized there was something inside one of them. She pulled out a narrow box in royal-blue velvet and opened it. Inside was a string

of pearls and hanging from it was a teardrop diamond surrounded by smaller diamonds.

She fastened it around her neck and gazed at herself in
the mirror.

Oh, my God. I'm a bride.

She sucked in a shaky breath then picked up her phone
and texted Kane.

Wait there a minute, he responded.

A moment later, there was a knock at the door. She
opened it, expecting to see Kane, but instead Will stood
there, wearing a tuxedo and holding a lovely bouquet of
pink and yellow roses. He was broad shouldered, tall, and
just as handsome as she remembered.

"Will. Hi."

He smiled. "Hello, River. I'm here to walk you down
the aisle."

As he handed her the bouquet, she realized the colors
of the roses were the same shades as the pink and yellow
in her mani, so it tied in nicely. Had Kane planned that?

"You look beautiful," Will said, a warm smile on his
face. He offered his elbow.

"Thank you." She hooked her arm in his. "You weren't
on the flight with us."

"No. I was in Chicago on business," he said as they
started to walk, "so as soon as Kane contacted me, I flew
out here to meet you."

He led her down the hall then stopped outside a double
door.

"Before we go in, I just wanted to say something."

She gazed up at him to see concern in his hazel eyes. "What is it?" she asked.

"Kane is my best friend and I love him deeply, but I also know that once he sets his mind on something, nothing stops him. I'm worried that in his exuberance, he might be pushing you a little faster than you want to go."

Man, there was an understatement.

But did Will think they were actually in love and that this was just a case of Kane rushing her to the altar?

"I know this might be overwhelming to you," he continued, "and that Kane has sworn you to secrecy about the arrangement, so I just want to let you know that if you ever want to talk, I'll be there for you."

"Oh, well . . . Thank you."

He smiled warmly. "Okay, are you ready?"

She smoothed down her dress and stared at the oak doors.

"As ready as I'll ever be."

Chapter Ten

At that, Will opened the doors. River drew in a breath at the sight of the beautiful stained-glass windows in the chapel with the setting sun glowing through. It was an ethereal sight. Organ music started and Will guided her down the aisle.

It felt almost like a real wedding.

As they walked past the wooden pews, her heart pumped faster. She couldn't believe this was happening. At the front of the chapel, there was a minister and the woman who had ushered them in. And Kane stood there watching her, looking incredibly handsome in his tuxedo.

When they reached him, Will took her hand and put it in Kane's then stepped to Kane's side. Her stomach tightened at the thought that there was no one here for her, but she pushed it aside. That's the way it was. No point stressing over it.

The minister started the ceremony and for some reason, tears welled in her eyes. She blinked them back, but too soon, they were saying their vows and her voice was strained, rasping from her closed throat as she said, "I do."

Kane rolled down the long glove on her left arm and drew it off. Then he slipped a ring on her finger. A sparkling band of diamonds. Her eyesight blurred a little as she stared at the glittering ring. He was so generous and kind and she knew he would treat her well, but—God, what was she doing? This whole thing was happening so fast her head was spinning.

She'd always dreamed of this day—standing at the front of a church, wearing a beautiful white gown . . . marrying the man of her dreams. One who loved and cherished her and wanted to be with her forever.

But that wasn't Kane. He didn't love her.

"You may kiss the bride."

Kane's arms came around her and their lips met. The kiss was persuasive and tender and when she opened her eyes as he drew away, she saw what she could almost believe was glowing happiness in his eyes. As if he were in love. But that was just her imagination, because it's what she wanted to see in her groom's eyes.

If only it were true.

Kane and Will walked her back to the room where she'd changed. She felt numb as she sat on the couch, waiting for them to leave so she could change back into her jeans.

"I thought we'd go for a celebratory drink," Kane said as he sat beside her.

Will sat in the chair angled toward the sofa.

A drink. Thank God. She certainly wasn't ready for
what would come after that.

Her wedding night.

"Oh, but all I have to wear are jeans," she said.

Kane nodded. "They won't be appropriate for where
we're going, so I had some dresses sent over. They should
be here any time now."

Within moments, someone knocked on the door and
Will answered it, then returned with a garment bag. He
hung it on the open door of the bathroom.

"Pick whichever one you like," Kane said as he stood
up. "Will and I will go change and meet you back here."

"Wait. First, I want to get a picture," Will said.

He pulled his cell phone from his pocket and snapped
a couple of pictures. Then Kane took a couple of pictures
of Will with River, insisting on having photos of his
bride and his best friend.

"Congratulations, Mrs. Winters," Will said.

He took her hand to shake it warmly. She turned her
head to smile at him, at the same time as he leaned in to
kiss her cheek, so his lips accidentally brushed hers. The
crackle of awareness that shot through her startled her.

She drew back.

"Thank you," she said quietly, barely able to speak,
dismayed by both the reminder that she was now Kane's
wife, and her surprising reaction to Will.

"We should get going," Kane said.

Once the two men left the room, she unzipped the bag
and pulled out the dresses. There were three, but the

purple wrap dress caught her eye. She loved the color, and it was almost the same color as the purple nail polish on her nails.

She slipped out of the wedding dress and pulled on the cocktail-length dress. It fit her perfectly, the wrap style accentuating her figure. She checked the bottom of the bag and found two pairs of shoes. One pair was black and the other pair was a perfect match for the purple. The latter were part suede and part smooth leather, with rhinestones edging the change in texture.

They had stiletto heels and when she stepped into them, she felt taller . . . and sexier.

There was even an evening bag in the same purple suede studded with rhinestones.

A knock sounded on the door just as she was moving her essentials from her purse to the small bag.

"Come in," she called.

The two men entered the room again, now wearing suits rather than the tuxes, but looking quite dashing. Kane's suit was black and he wore a purple tie that matched her dress.

He smiled. "The personal shopper told me she'd sent two black dresses and a purple dress. I knew you'd choose that one."

"And it looks great with your nails," Will said. "That's quite the manicure."

"Thanks," she said, unable to hold back a smile at his compliment.

She was used to people like Louise who disapproved

of her creative abandon. She glanced at Kane, but could tell nothing from his expression. Did that include him?

Kane offered his arm.

"First, I need you to undo the necklace. I couldn't get the clasp undone." She lifted her long hair—still in a ponytail—out of the way as she turned her back to Kane.

"Don't you like the necklace?" he asked.

"Of course. It's lovely."

He rested his hands on her shoulders and turned her around to face him. She released her hair, and it swished across her back.

"I just assumed you'd be sending it back."

"Sending it back where?" Kane asked.

Her finger slid to the large teardrop diamond.

"I don't know. I assumed you just gave it to me for the wedding."

"It was a gift. As was the wedding dress, the shoes, the dress you're wearing now."

"Oh . . ." She gazed up at him. "But . . . are they real diamonds?"

He smiled. "Of course."

"I'm not sure if I'm comfortable—"

"Accepting a gift from your husband?"

She gazed up at him.

Kane is my husband.

Her knees felt weak. *How did I let this happen?*

"I'm just . . . what if they got stolen?"

"Then I'd buy you something new."

She drew in a breath, feeling overwhelmed. She wasn't

used to getting gifts from men. And certainly not expensive gifts like diamonds. She wanted to be gracious, but . . . they were so extravagant and . . . they weren't her.

She glanced at the glittering wedding band. Except that. It was simple and lovely.

"Now let's go for that drink." Kane offered his arm again. She wrapped her fingers around it.

"What about my clothes and . . . the other things?"

"Someone will take care of that for us," Kane answered as he led her from the room.

Will leaned in close. "Don't worry. Now that you've married into money, you'll get used to having other people handle that kind of thing."

Her back stiffened. Did Will think she'd married Kane just because he was rich? Her cheeks flushed as she realized that *was* why she'd married him. Maybe it wasn't just to relax and live off his money, but it *was* because of his investment . . . and his connections.

From Will's comment earlier, he knew Kane had sworn her to secrecy about the arrangement, so he must know that it was a business deal of sorts between her and Kane. Her cheeks heated more. Did he think she was a gold digger, selling her body to advance her business?

A limo was waiting for them at the door and she slid inside, followed by Kane, then Will. Ten minutes later, the limo pulled into the entrance of a hotel. As she got out of the car, the skirt of the wrap dress revealed a long expanse of thigh. She quickly stood up and smoothed it down, but she'd seen the heat in Kane's eyes as his gaze had lingered.

And that reminded her that after these drinks, he would take her to a hotel room and they'd consummate this marriage. His hands would glide over her naked skin. He'd kiss her and touch her in intimate places. Anxiety skittered through her along with shimmers of heated desire.

A uniformed man held the door open for them and they crossed the bright, noisy lobby to an elevator. When the doors opened to a lounge, it was quieter. Softly lit and carpeted, with a spectacular view of the Strip. The hostess led them to a window seat. The sun had set and the sky was streaked with orange and purple as the sunlight slowly faded and the city lights became brighter.

A waitress in a short, tight dress, cut low in front showing her ample cleavage, delivered a bottle of champagne to the table. She popped the cork and filled three glasses.

"You know, you were the one that got away," Will said. "The one he talked about incessantly, wondering what might have been. Well, he finally trapped you," he said with a wink, "and I truly hope you find happiness together." He raised his glass. "To a happy life together."

River raised her champagne and they all clinked glasses. She sipped the bubbly liquid, barely tasting it.

Kane watched his new bride. Her face had gone pale when Will made the toast and he was pretty sure she was imagining a bleak future with him. She must be feeling panicky and pressured, and probably second-guessing the rush decision.

Not that he was. He was glad he'd been able to talk her into this before she had a chance to really think it through. Because he was bound and determined to convince her that they could be happy together.

He sipped his champagne as she and Will talked. He was really glad the two of them were hitting it off. They were the two most important people in his life.

The awkward, accidental half kiss between them had surprised Kane, because he thought he'd seen a spark between them. But it was probably nothing. And even if there was something there, he trusted Will with his life. He knew Will would never take what was Kane's.

"Do you have a girlfriend, Will?" River asked.

Will's gaze shifted to Kane, then down to his glass.

"No. I was seeing someone, but it ended recently."

River frowned. "I'm sorry." Her fingertips brushed hesitantly over his hand, but then she drew them away.

"Don't worry about Will," Kane said. "He's resilient."

Will's gaze shifted to Kane again, but he nodded and sipped his wine.

"That's right. It was a casual thing that had been going on for some time. We're still friends."

"Friends with benefits?" she asked.

Will stared at his glass and Kane's chest tightened at the sadness in his eyes.

"No, I'm afraid not."

"You know," Kane said, anxious to change the subject, "Will suggested you two meet and talk about your business. He thought he might have some ideas to help you with production."

"Well, production is pretty much mixing pigment with the base, adding things like glitter or flakies, and pouring it all into the bottles."

"I'm sure you know what you're doing," Will said. "I just thought I might be able to help you streamline the process. Or maybe build something that helps, like shaking the bottles."

"I don't think at this point I—"

Kane placed his hand on hers. "He just wants to help, River. You're totally in charge, okay?"

"That's right." Will sat back. "We can do it whenever you want. Or not at all. I'm at your disposal."

Her gaze flickered to Kane, then back to Will. "Thank you. I'll keep that in mind."

She lifted her glass to sip the champagne and the glitter of the candlelight on the diamonds in her wedding band reminded him of the velvet box in his pocket.

He pulled it out. "I almost forgot to give you this."

He set the brown velvet box on the table. She picked it up and opened it. He had hoped her eyes would light up at the sight of the marquis-cut diamond solitaire ring, but she just stared at it, wide-eyed.

"Another gift?"

"It's an engagement ring. I know our engagement was pretty short, but . . ." He pulled the ring from its soft cushion of velvet and took her hand, then slid it on her finger. "That doesn't mean you shouldn't have a ring."

It looked beautiful on her long, slender finger.

She glanced at Will nervously. Of course, she'd be wondering if he knew yet.

"River, I've already told Will about our arrangement."

She nodded, her cheeks staining a deep crimson and her gaze locked on her glass. She sipped deeply.

"It's okay. He's not judging in any way."

Will chuckled. "And if I was, it'd be Kane I'm judging."

Kane knew Will was making light of it to relax River, but Will had tried to talk him out of his plan. He'd thought Kane was crazy to force her into this, but he also knew that Kane always succeeded when he set his mind to something.

Will had other reasons to be unhappy, too, but he'd been supportive, knowing how much Kane needed to be with River. Knowing how long he'd been pining for her.

Kane poured River another glass of champagne.

He would make this work. He'd win her over.

And it all started tonight.

River stood beside Kane as he pushed the key card into the door then opened it. He rested his hand on the small of her back, as if he thought she might flee, and guided her into the room.

But it wasn't simply a room. It was a huge, luxurious suite.

The first thing she saw was a sitting area with a couch and chairs arranged in front of floor-to-ceiling windows.

There was a bar on one wall and a dining area beyond with a table and chairs for six. On the table was an ice bucket with champagne, tall flutes, and a basket of fruit.

And candles. The whole suite was bathed in the soft glow of dozens of candles. The chandelier over the dining table and the lamps were dimmed so the flickering flames set a soft, romantic mood. Soft music played in the background.

Her stomach clenched. This was her wedding night. It was time to consummate the marriage.

She stood hesitantly, but Kane guided her farther into the room.

"Don't worry. I'm not just going to throw you down on the bed and take you."

Chapter Eleven

"No, I didn't think that," River said.

He gestured to the couch and she sat down.

"Are you sure? Because your expression says otherwise." He slipped off his suit jacket and laid it on the arm of a chair.

"I assumed we'd have champagne first," she quipped.

He laughed. "Would you like some champagne?" He walked to the table and pulled the bottle from the ice.

"Yes, please."

She noticed a gift-wrapped box—about the size of a small throw cushion—on one of the armchairs. This one was wrapped in ivory paper with a delicate tone-on-tone design, and tied with a big, red satin bow.

"Don't tell me that's another gift for me."

He glanced at the box as he unwrapped the cork.

"No. That one's really more for me."

Her cheeks heated.

"But don't worry about that right now. Let's just

relax." He popped the cork. "There's fruit here. And the basket has some chocolate."

"Chocolate?"

He laughed and carried the two flutes in one hand and the bottle of champagne and a small box of chocolates in the other. He set everything on the coffee table in front of her, then filled the two glasses and handed her one.

He slipped the gift behind the chair, out of sight. He clearly realized the thought of slipping into skimpy lingerie made her uncomfortable and he was being sensitive to her needs. The thought made her relax a little more.

He sat down beside her and opened the box of chocolates. She sipped the bubbly liquid and set her glass down.

"Here, try this." He held a chocolate close to her mouth.

She opened and he fed it to her. The brush of his fingertips against her lips sent shivers through her.

The smooth, dark chocolate melted in her mouth and she tasted sweet, creamy orange. She enjoyed the delectable treat as it dissolved on her tongue, and then she swallowed.

"Mmm. I love orange cream chocolates."

"Damn. I wish I'd been the one to make your face glow like that."

She gazed at him and saw the desire in his eyes.

Her heart rate increased.

They'd been together before—in fact, she'd been the assertive one that time—but now . . . after so many years . . . after what had happened between them . . .

She stared at her hand sitting on her lap and the diamonds sparkling on her finger. But now she was his wife.

And he was trying to make this night special.

She gazed into his indigo eyes, seeing a deep craving there. She tipped up her face and leaned toward him. He met her, his lips brushing hers. Lightly. She pressed her tongue into his mouth, stroking. He could probably taste the chocolate.

He stroked her tongue in return, then drew back and his eyes glittered in the candlelight as his hand curled around her cheek and jaw.

"We don't have to rush this."

She nodded then picked up her glass and sipped again.

"Would you like me to change?" she asked. "Maybe check out what's in the box behind the chair?"

"What I want is for you to be comfortable and I sense that I've overwhelmed you."

"But this is our wedding night and if you bought that for me . . ."

"It's okay." He took her hand and lifted it to his mouth. The light brush of his lips on her skin made her shiver.

She cleared her throat. "The chocolates are good. You should try one."

He smiled. "Sure." But he didn't reach for the box.

She got the hint and selected one then brought it to his mouth. He opened and she placed it inside. His lips closed around the tip of her finger, sending goose bumps dancing along her arm. She watched his lips move a little as he enjoyed the candy. She could imagine it in his mouth.

The rich chocolate smooth and sweet . . . melting . . . coating his tongue.

She couldn't help herself. She leaned in close and pressed her mouth to his and ran her tongue along the seam of his lips. They parted and she nudged inside, tasting the sweetness of the chocolate. His was raspberry. Tasting the chocolate on his tongue was delightfully sweet and sexy.

She started to draw away, having indulged more than she'd intended, but his arms came around her and he held her close, then sucked on her tongue, drawing it deeper into his mouth. Her heart pounded as the heady delight of the chocolate, and the feel of his tongue gliding into her mouth overwhelmed her senses.

Finally, his arms loosened and she drew away, a little reluctantly.

"You like chocolate," he said in his deep, silky voice.

"I do."

The two words reminded her why they were here and she flushed. This was their wedding night and they were here to seal the deal.

The soft romantic song that had been playing ended and another song started. She recognized it as "Breathe" by Faith Hill, a song she really loved.

He took her hand and stood up.

"Come and dance with me."

She stood and he guided her to a clear area on the carpet. Then his arms swept around her and he drew her close to his body. It was overwhelming, being enveloped in his arms, his masculine presence all around her.

She rested her head against his shoulder as they moved to the music. It was like floating . . . him guiding her through the air as if on a cloud.

Oh, God, she'd had too much champagne and was light-headed.

She relaxed against him, deciding not to fight it. Letting her cares drift away.

She could feel him breathe. The rise and fall of his chest. The gentle rush of air across her temple.

She sighed and melted against him. Caught up in his closeness. In his touch.

The desire—so long suppressed—came rushing through her.

Baby, isn't that the way that love's supposed to be.

She sighed. She wanted him like she'd never wanted another man.

. . . all the walls come tumbling down.

She wanted to love him. To really be his wife.

She nuzzled his neck, dragging her teeth along the light shadow of bristles on his jaw. He tucked his finger under her chin and tipped up her head. Then his lips met hers. They continued moving to the music, his mouth coaxing hers, as the song washed through her, inciting a mélange of emotions.

She started to unbutton his shirt, running her fingers down the smooth skin of his chest as the shirt parted. He

tugged off his tie and tossed it aside as her fingers continued their journey.

She pressed her lips to the pulse point at the base of
his neck, feeling the blood pumping through him. Feeling it quicken. She pushed his shirt off his shoulders, and
drew it down his arms until it fell to the floor.

He untied her dress, his trailing fingertips gliding
along the bare skin of her stomach, and she drew the sleeves
down her arms and let the garment slip away.

Now she stood before him in her bra and panties, and
the garter belt and stockings he'd given her. She wished
she'd worn something white and lacy that would look
nice with the lacy white garter belt—something more
bridal. But he didn't seem to mind, gazing at her lavender
bra and panties hungrily.

"Maybe I should go put on what you have in the box."

"No." He stroked her shoulder, gliding the strap of her
bra to one side. "I like you just the way you are." Then he
scooped her up and carried her to the bedroom.

Candles filled that room, too, and the bed was already
turned down, so he set her on the pristine white sheets.
He stepped back and unfastened his pants, then let them
drop to the floor. A second later, his boxers were gone,
too.

She gazed at his towering erection, her insides quivering.

She wanted him. Oh, God, it was a desperate ache
deep inside her that threatened to tear her apart if she didn't
satisfy it.

She reached out her hand. "Come here. Please."

He stepped closer and she wrapped her hand around his pulsing shaft as soon as he was within reach. He sat on the bed beside her as she stroked his cock, the soft flesh gliding over the hard column beneath. He unfastened her bra and slipped it away as she stared at his erection, loving the feel of it, thick and hard within her grasp.

She slid to the floor and knelt in front of him. He stroked her breast, enveloping it in his hand as she nuzzled the tip of him. Pleasure quivered through her at his touch.

She'd missed this. Her hand stroked his length. She'd dreamed of doing this so many times.

He stroked back her hair as she wrapped her lips around his cockhead and enveloped him in her mouth. Her tongue flickered under the crown . . . teasing . . . then she swirled over the tip in circles.

"Oh, sweetheart."

She loved the need in his voice. She stroked him with her hand as she sucked, then glided deeper. She tucked her other hand beneath his balls and stroked them gently. She sucked harder, and then glided up and down his shaft, loving the feel of it twitching . . . the sound of his soft groan.

She slid off his tip, continuing to pump his cock with her hand.

"Do you want me, Kane?"

His fingers glided through her hair, then tucked around her head.

"Fuck, yes, sweetheart."

His words thrilled her.

She stuffed his cockhead in her mouth again and sucked deeply, caressing his balls at the same time.

"Show me. Come in my mouth right now."

She pushed him back between her lips, stroking his shaft quickly. At the same time, she tweaked one of her nipples, and kept toying with it as he watched her, his eyes the color of midnight.

Then he sucked in a breath and she felt it, the semen pulsing through his shaft, then flooding into her mouth. She sucked and squeezed him, urging him on. He groaned, the flow continuing for another few seconds, and then his hand loosened on her head.

"Oh, God, baby. That was something."

He drew her onto his lap and took her lips, the passion of his kiss stunning her. His tongue swept into her mouth and she met it eagerly.

He turned and laid her on the bed then kissed down her neck and nuzzled that place right at the base that drove her wild. She glided her fingers through his thick wavy hair, her pulse racing. Then he continued down her shoulder. His hand glided over her breast, then his lips found her swollen, tingling nipple and he took it in his mouth. When he suckled, she moaned, pulling him tighter against her.

He chuckled then his lips danced lightly down her stomach. When he settled between her thighs, leaning on his elbows and gazing up at her, her stomach fluttered in anticipation. He stroked a fingertip along the top edge of her lavender lace panties. Playfully, he dipped a finger underneath and lifted the elastic, then peered inside.

He glided the panties down, slowly revealing her intimate flesh. He flicked them down her legs and dropped them on the floor, then pressed her knees wider apart.

"Your pussy looks so damn sweet." He smiled at her. "It's a little different than I remember it."

She flushed as she remembered she had been au naturel when they'd been together last.

He dragged a finger along the naked folds and she trembled in delight.

He leaned forward and pressed his mouth to her petals of flesh. When his tongue swept over her, she drew in a breath. His thumbs stroked the sides of her folds while he dipped his tongue inside her. Her eyelids fluttered closed. He glided a finger inside and stroked her passage. Soon he slid another finger into her opening and the feel of his fingertips, glazed with her wetness, gliding deeper, filled her with need. She arched against his mouth.

He found her clit and lapped at it. The sensitive bundle of nerves almost seemed to vibrate with pleasure, sending heated waves of delight washing through her. He lapped again and she moaned.

Then he suckled and pleasure rippled through her . . . rising like the tide . . . overwhelming her senses . . . until she gasped, then moaned as sparks flared behind her eyelids. She tossed her head back and forth, crying out in ecstasy.

His mouth continued to move on her as the orgasm

waned, then he lifted his head and gazed at her . . . the look on his face tender and possessive.

She opened her arms to him and he prowled over her. His body settled on hers as he kissed her with passion.

She glided her hand down his body, seeking his penis. When she found it, it was hard and ready for her. Thick and heavy in her hand. And pulsing with need.

She pressed it to her slick opening and he nudged forward.

Oh, God, yes . . . she needed him inside her with an intensity that was almost frightening.

He wrapped his hand around his cock, over hers, and glided it along her slit, sending shivers of desire through her.

"I need you," she murmured. "Please fill me."

He kissed her neck, tingles dancing through her at the light brush of his lips.

"I will, sweetheart. Whatever you want is yours."

He pressed forward and his cockhead stretched her. Wider. His thick shaft slowly pushing deeper. Stretching her narrow opening.

"Oh, yes," she whimpered, stunned at how potent the sensations were. At how intensely she craved him.

He pushed deeper, her flesh gripping him tightly.

He nuzzled her ear, sending goose bumps along her neck. "You're so tight."

She nipped his earlobe. "Fill me," she insisted.

He surged deeper. She squeezed around his thick shaft and he groaned, and then slid all the way in.

She clung to him, holding him tight to her body. His hard chest against her sensitive, swollen nipples. Her breasts crushed flat.

She rocked her pelvis against him, delightful sensations fluttering through her as the angle of his hard shaft shifted inside her.

She rocked again. This time, he groaned.

But he lay still, his hard body against hers, her fingernails digging into his back.

"Sweetheart, how many men have you been with since me?"

Chapter Twelve

Oh, God, why did he have to ask her that?

River shrugged. "About two dozen," she lied.

Kane's eyebrow lifted. "Two *dozen*?"

Clearly, that was too many.

"I mean about a dozen."

The way the light danced in his eyes, she didn't think he believed her. But she didn't want to tell him it had only been a couple.

He nuzzled her neck. "I had rather hoped you'd say none. That I had ruined you for other men."

Her stomach clenched. That was too close to the truth, but she would never let him know that.

She dug her fingernails deeper into his back, desperately wishing he'd just fuck her again.

But she couldn't help asking, "What about you?"

A flicker in his eyes—of doubt or sadness—caught her off guard.

But he grinned and said, "How about I say two dozen, too?"

Then he began to move. Slowly. His cock dragging along her slick canal. Lighting a fire within her. Then he glided deep again.

Then out.

Then deep again.

"Ohhh, Kane."

He nuzzled her neck. "Sweetheart, I want you to come for me."

She nodded, her breath locked in her chest as his cock drove deep.

He filled her again and again, pleasure rising inside her. Swelling through her whole being.

Everything centered on his moving shaft. Pleasure rippling in its wake.

She squeezed, intensifying the sensations. He groaned and thrust faster.

Deeper.

"Oh, yeah." She met every thrust with a rise of her hips, driving him even deeper still.

Joyful sensations coiled inside her, then like a flash flood, exploded through her body. She clung to him, gasping, as the orgasm tore through her.

Still he thrust.

The orgasm waned, followed by another, cresting even higher.

"Oh, Kane, I'm . . . ohhh."

"Am I making you come again, baby?" he murmured against her ear.

She nodded, and then moaned. Her mind and body expanded as one, attuned in a total state of bliss.

Kane drove hard, groaning, and then erupted inside her.

He held her tight to his body as they both gasped for air. She dug her fingers into his back, never wanting to let him go.

Their breathing slowed and finally he rolled to his side.

He kissed her cheek then rested his face close to hers.

She gazed into his indigo eyes, loving how close he was. Wishing he was still inside her body.

He smiled. "I must say, this arrangement is working out very nicely."

Oh, God, oh, God, oh, God.

Kane was asleep. His arm was around her waist and his body pressed the length of her back.

River tried not to rock to console herself—she didn't want to wake him up—but his words kept echoing in her head.

I must say, this arrangement is working out very nicely.

She was an arrangement. A contract.

A convenient lover.

He'd been so sweet. So tender. Everything had been so romantic.

But of course he'd want to have things go smoothly during their first time together. That didn't mean he was in love with her. In fact, ever since Will had told her she was the one who got away, she'd worried that he wanted her only because she was the one thing he couldn't have, and that now that he had her, he would soon lose interest.

She bit her lip. The problem was . . . the way she'd felt in his arms tonight . . . the way she'd hungered for him ever since that first time so many years ago . . .

She knew . . . deep in her heart . . . her chest tightened . . . that she did love *him*.

Oh, God, he might be her husband, but he would never love her.

A deep loneliness filled her soul. She'd always been a misfit and now . . . She choked back a sob. Now she was a misfit in her own marriage.

Tears spilled from her eyes, but she swiped them away. She would not cry. She would not succumb to the deep melancholy that haunted her. She would make this work. She had walked into this marriage with her eyes open and she couldn't blame this on Kane or anyone else.

She'd made her bed and now she was sleeping in it.

With Kane.

His arm flexed in his sleep, drawing her a little tighter to him.

Things could be worse.

Kane would take care of her, and help her with her business. As independent as she had always been, there was something seductive about the idea of someone taking care of her for a change. Someone she could depend on. It was more than she'd ever had from her father or mother.

She'd just have to remember what this arrangement really was and try to keep her heart safe.

In the morning, River turned to find Kane's face on the pillow only inches from her own. His eyes were open and he smiled.

"Good morning, Mrs. Winters."

"Hi," she said in a sleepy voice.

Sunlight streamed in the window. It was a beautiful day out.

"I ordered breakfast to be sent up to the room." He stroked her shoulder lightly, sending tingles through her. He gave her that heart-stopping smile. "But we have a little time."

She wanted to. *Oh, God,* she wanted to. But she just didn't want to be the good wife this morning. She needed a breather.

"I don't think so, I"—she shrugged—"need to use the ladies' room."

He rolled onto his back. "Believe me, I can wait."

At the sight of the tent pole under the covers, her eyes widened. Was this what it was going to be like every day? Waking up beside him? Him so clearly wanting her?

It made her feel . . . needed.

And how pathetic was that? Any woman would meet his needs. It wasn't *her* he wanted.

Except for the chemistry between them. That, at least, did make her special.

She sat up, holding the sheets against her chest, wanting to pull them from the bed, but he tugged, loosening her grasp.

"You're being exceptionally shy this morning," he teased.

He was right, she was being silly. She released the sheets and stood up.

Oh, God, that was a mistake. The heat in his eyes as his gaze seared down her body took her breath away. She turned and hurried to the bathroom before even her full bladder wouldn't stop her from climbing right back into bed with him.

A few minutes later, as she was opening the shower stall door, she heard a knock on the door.

"Sweetheart, breakfast is here."

"I'm just about to take a shower," she called to him.

She heard the door open and she turned around.

"That sounds like an invitation to me."

"I . . ." But the sight of him dropping his robe to the floor, his cock swelling and rising, caught her breath.

He guided her into the shower stall, which was the size of the whole bathroom in her apartment. He turned on the water, then pressed her to the wall and kissed her.

"It'll take a minute for it to heat up," he said.

With the way he was looking at her, and the feel of his cock pressing against her belly, it took no time at all for *her* to heat up.

His hand stroked down her side and rested on her hip. She couldn't help it. Her hand glided down his chest then over his sculpted abs until her fingertips trailed over his cock. She wrapped her hand around it.

There was a bench on one end of the stall, so she pressed him toward it. The water washed over them—warm and soothing—as she guided him to sit down. She stood in front of him and he stroked her breasts, then his lips found her nipple and he took it in his mouth. Pleasure seeped through her and she could feel the moisture pooling between her thighs.

She knelt on the bench facing him, her legs on either side of him, then pressed his cock to her opening. Once it was in position, she wrapped her arms around him and kissed him, driving her tongue into his mouth as she slowly lowered herself onto his hard-as-rock cock. She moaned into his mouth as it filled her. Stretching her. Pushing deep inside. While warm water rained down all around her.

Once he was all the way in, she sat facing him for a moment. His gaze locked with hers and she thought she saw . . . could it be that he . . . ?

He grasped her hips and lifted, then lowered her again. All thoughts scattered at the feel of that marble shaft moving inside her.

Her head tipped back, the water streaming through her long hair as he glided into her body in a steady rhythm.

She squeezed him, loving the feel of him inside her.

"Ohhh, Kane." The pleasure soared within her and she

gasped. "I'm going to . . ." Bliss swelled inside her, her whole body a tingling mass of sensation.

"Oh, fuck, baby. Me, too."

Then they both groaned in a simultaneous, wildly explosive orgasm, the tiled stall filled with the echo of their passion.

His hands on her hips slowed, until finally she settled on his lap, the two of them staring into each other's eyes. She sucked in deep breaths, her heart still pounding from the intensity of the experience.

He simply stared back, looking as stunned as she felt.

Then he kissed her neck.

"We should finish our shower and go get breakfast before it gets cold."

After breakfast, they packed up and checked out. Will met them at the waiting limo, which took them to the airport.

"So the honeymoon's over," Will teased, as he sat beside River on the plane. "Now back to the real world."

The real world.

River shivered. She had no idea what that was anymore. Certainly, her life had changed radically. And that thought was hammered home when they pulled up in front of a luxury apartment building.

She was surprised when Kane got out of the car and offered his hand.

"We're not going to your house?" she asked as she walked toward the entrance with Kane and Will.

"No, I just go there on weekends and whenever I want

to entertain," Kane said. "Will and I both have apartments here."

A doorman held the door open for them and they entered the vast, luxurious lobby.

"You can't entertain at your apartment?" She hadn't seen it yet, but judging from his student apartment, and his current house, she was sure it would be stunning.

He shrugged as they stepped onto the elevator.

"The house makes a better impression. Of stability. Class. It's what's expected."

"And that's important to you?"

He shrugged. "To a certain extent. Especially in business."

She stared down at the glittering rings he'd given her, then at her bright, multicolored mani. He'd probably prefer she wear something more subdued. Maybe a deep red, or even something neutral like a nude. And what would he think of her wardrobe?

If he had a house specifically to entertain in, he must host parties and she'd be his hostess. Would he expect her to dress a certain way? Behave a certain way?

Will leaned in and nudged her elbow. "He may sound like a stuck-up prig, but we both love him anyway," he said with a grin.

"Yeah, thanks, buddy," Kane said with a hint of sarcasm.

The elevator stopped on floor eighteen.

"Well, see you later," Will said as he stepped into the carpeted hallway.

The doors closed and the elevator started moving again.

She frowned. "Why do you care about what other people think?"

He shrugged. "What other people think of you can help you or hurt you in life. It's important, and anyone who says otherwise is just fooling themselves."

"Then why did you marry me? I won't fit in your upscale world."

"You're a beautiful, talented woman. You'll do fine."

Was he saying she was a trophy wife? But she knew better. If that's what he'd wanted, he could attract any number of stunning women who would fit far better into his world than she ever would.

"And if I wasn't?"

He smiled and slid his arm around her waist, drawing her close. "Look, I love the person you are. Your creativity. Your quirkiness. I'm just saying that you have those other assets, too. And as my wife, I know you'll want to make a good impression when we're out with people where it matters."

"And who *matters*?" she asked with gritted teeth, leaning away from him.

His arm loosened around her and slid away.

"I just mean contacts who could affect my standing in the business or social community. Just as I'll act appropriately to help you with your business."

The elevator doors opened and she strode out, not caring that she didn't know which direction to go. But it didn't matter because she walked right into a huge penthouse apartment. She slowed as the view from the floor-to-ceiling windows caught her eye. She held her breath as she stopped at the window, gazing out the glass at the sight of the river glistening in the sunlight below. And the park along its banks.

"It's . . . beautiful."

He stepped to her side and gazed out with her. "I like it." He took her elbow. "Come on, I'll show you the place."

It became a blur as he took her from lavish room to lavish room. The kitchen gleamed with shiny granite counters, glossy hardwood floors, and rich, dark cabinets. The living room was all light-colored leather and the same dark wood as the kitchen.

"There are three bedrooms, but one is my den."

Her back stiffened. Was he going to put her in the second bedroom? It made sense. She was here to satisfy his sexual needs, but that didn't mean they needed to sleep together. He might want his own space.

And that was fine with her. Better, in fact.

But he pushed open the double doors at the end of the hall and rolled her suitcase into it. When she glanced inside, and realized this was clearly the master bedroom, she relaxed a little. She'd been lying to herself. It might be better for her sanity to have her own room, but being in his room with him made her feel more . . . wanted.

"Can we go to my place and pick up some of my things?" she asked.

"No need." He led her to a door and opened it. On

the other side was a huge walk-in closet filled with dark-stained, solid wood furniture with brass fittings. There were drawers, shelves, closed cupboards, and lots of space to hang clothes.

Then she saw her clothes hanging alongside his.

"I had someone move your things in this morning."

"People went through my stuff? And packed it up and brought it here?"

"You can't tell me you really wanted to do that yourself."

No, she hated moving. "But . . . my stuff is private."

He shrugged. "It's not like the people doing it would care. They do this all the time. You don't have anything that would surprise them."

"That's not the point," she flared. "It's my stuff. I don't like the idea of anyone going through my stuff."

"I'm sorry. I'm used to people handling that kind of thing for me. I never even thought of it being an issue."

He took her hand. "You aren't going to hold this against me, are you? After we've gotten off to such a good start?" He squeezed her fingers. "I just wanted you to feel at home right away."

His smile—designed to charm—succeeded.

She nodded. "Okay. Thank you. It was very thoughtful."

"Good." He kissed her, a gentle kiss on the lips. "Now, in addition to this space"—he gestured to where her clothes were hanging—"you've also got that dresser. And if you need more space, we'll accommodate that."

She stared at the dresser he indicated, which had six big drawers.

"I'm sure my stuff only takes up half of that thing."

"But you'll be getting more clothes. Things better suited to your new life."

"My new life?" she echoed.

"Well, let's face it. You had to live on a budget. And you did a great job. But now you can get some quality items. I'm setting up an appointment for you with my personal shopper and she can help you pick out some things."

She frowned. "I think what I have is fine."

But she glanced at her dresses, pants, skirts, and blouses hanging up beside his finely tailored suits. His clothes were clearly custom made and of the highest quality whereas she shopped at the Goodwill store. She loved doing that—she got some amazing finds and it allowed her creativity to shine. But when she looked at her clothes hanging side by side with his, it was like one of those puzzles: what doesn't fit here?

He smiled. "You can't honestly be turning down the offer of new clothes."

She didn't care about fancy clothes. She honestly loved her wardrobe. Every piece meant something to her. But she had agreed to be his wife and that meant making some concessions.

"You already bought me that nice dress for drinks last night, but if you don't think that's enough for going out to special places, I could get a few more things. But I can pick out my own clothes."

"Of course you'll have a say, but it'll be easier if you go with her. She'll take you around to the right stores, ensure everything fits just right, and I'll ask her to arrange a whole makeover for you. Hair, makeup. Everything. I'm sure she could do it tomorrow afternoon."

She just stared at him, flabbergasted. Wasn't there anything he liked about the way she looked?

"What do you mean, you're married?"

River bit her lip as she stared at Tia's shocked expression.

"It was pretty fast."

"Fast? I didn't even know you were seeing anyone. The last guy you went out with was . . ." Tia's eyes widened. "Nooo! It's not the billionaire? That guy from your past?"

River bit back the retort that it hadn't been a date. She was supposed to be selling this to Tia.

"But you said . . ." Tia shook her head. "I mean, I thought you hated him."

"I did. For a long time. But when I went back to talk to him like you suggested, he explained what happened back in college." She shook her head. "It wasn't his fault. His friends were responsible for the whole thing, and neither of us knew."

Tia's eyes narrowed. "Why didn't he tell you that in college?" she asked doubtfully.

"I left school after what happened—I mean, it was the end of the school year anyway, but I didn't go back—and he didn't know how to find me, so we were never able to talk things out. But he said he never forgot me and he finally realized he was in love with me." That last part was how River wished things had happened. "Then when he saw my Kickstarter campaign, he used that to get in touch with me again. And although I was really angry at him, I never forgot that night with him, and what it was like. When he explained what really happened . . ." She shrugged. "Well, you know what they say about love and hate being two sides of the same coin."

"Okay, I know I was a little inebriated when you told me the story of what happened between you two," Tia said, looking a little more convinced, "but I remember you saying he was your first. And that he was perfect. But then you said something about it all being a lie."

"Well, that's because he . . . uh . . . went out with me on a bet." The oversimplified summary sounded weak. But there was no way she'd tell Tia about the rest of the humiliation.

"He slept with you on a bet? Oh, that's harsh."

River nodded. "The fact that he didn't really want to be with me . . . really hurt . . . you know?"

Tia patted her hand. "Of course. He seemed so nice, but any man who would do that . . ."

Oh, no, this was going in the wrong direction.

"No, he said that sleeping with me wasn't part of the bet." And part of her clung to the belief that that was really true. "That he had already started falling for me by that point and really wanted to be with me."

"And you believe that's true?"

River gazed straight at Tia and summoned her most convincing voice. "Yes, I do. Would I have married him otherwise?"

"Okay. As long as you're sure, I'm happy for you."

They gazed at each other a little longer and a smile blossomed on Tia's face.

"Oh, God, River. You're really married," Tia said in awe, and then she grabbed her and hugged her tight. "I'm so happy for you." She eased off on the tight hug and sat back. "Now let me see the ring."

Tia grabbed River's hand and stared at the glittering diamond.

"Oh, my God, it's huge! You lucky girl." Tia's smile glowed. "So tell me about the wedding."

"We did a quick trip to Vegas."

"You went to *Vegas*?" The pitch of Tia's voice had increased a notch. "And you didn't invite me? I've never been and I've always wanted to go."

River squeezed Tia's hand. "Oh, Tia, I wanted you there. I'll make it up to you somehow."

After spending the afternoon with Maggie, Kane's personal shopper, River returned to the penthouse with a ton of bags. The doorman insisted on bringing them to the apartment for her, so she grabbed just a couple of the bags and walked to the elevator while he arranged for the rest.

As the elevator glided upward, she glanced at her reflection in the mirrored walls, not quite recognizing herself. Maggie had taken her to a salon and the stylist had dyed her hair, so now rather than the deep burgundy color, her hair was done in a trendy tortoiseshell ombré, with her natural dark brown mixed with multiple golden tones, deeper at the roots and lighter at the ends. They'd left her hair long, but layered it to add more fullness.

They'd shown her how to do her makeup to go well with her hair, showing off her green eyes with warm, smoky shades. She had to admit, the look suited her, but it left her not feeling like herself.

The doors opened and she stepped off the elevator. A large suitcase stood in the entryway.

Chapter Thirteen

River's first thought was that Kane had had second thoughts and was sending her on her way, but she realized she was just being silly.

"There you are." Kane walked from the hallway into the living room, file folders in his hand. "Did you have a good time?" He walked to his desk where his briefcase stood open, with barely a glance her way.

"Yes, I guess so."

He laughed as he placed the folders into the case. "You're the only woman I know who isn't thrilled by a shopping trip." He added a few more things from his desk, then closed the case and glanced her way. Then his eyes lit up.

"Well, hello. You look stunning."

Besides her new makeup and hair, she wore a new dress in emerald green, long with a slim line that made her look taller and slimmer than she'd ever thought possible.

The matching shoes, with their four-inch heels, helped a lot, too.

She loved the dress, and the shoes, but it was a little conservative for her. But the way it made her feel—sexy and very feminine had convinced her to buy it, at Maggie's urging, of course.

Now with the way Kane was looking at her, she thought she might never take it off.

Heat thrummed through her. Unless he suggested it.

He walked toward her, his heated gaze lingering on her body, a slow smile spreading across his face.

He slid his fingers through her thick mane of hair and cupped her head, then drew her in for a kiss. His lips were coaxing on hers and she opened to allow his tongue to glide inside.

She wrapped her arms around him, realizing she'd missed him, even though she'd been gone only a few hours. His kiss grew more passionate and desire quivered through her. She wanted to strip off the dress and feel his hands all over her body. She wanted to stroke his solid muscles and feel his hard cock slide inside her.

Oh, God, he was becoming addictive.

Their tongues curled around each other, and then he drew hers into his mouth and suckled lightly, igniting a deeper need in her.

Then he drew away.

"I can't tell you how much I want to continue this, but I'm afraid I can't."

"Why not?" she asked in surprise.

He smiled, as if happy at her disappointment. "I have to go out of town. There's a chain of Italian boutiques expanding their market into the U.S., and if the meeting goes well, I'll be one of their biggest investors. I don't want to get your hopes up, but it might even lead to more distribution opportunities for your nail polish, down the road, of course. I'm sorry to do this so soon, but it can't be helped."

"That's wonderful! Can I go with you?"

His smile grew broader. "I would love that, but I'll be gone a week and I assume you'll need that time to get started on your nail polish if you're going to meet the deadline for Rapture."

"Oh, right." Disappointment washed through her.

"I believe your supplies have arrived. A card was delivered to your old apartment today saying there's a box waiting for you. I've arranged for someone to pick it up."

He cupped her face and gave her another light kiss. "Will is going to come by tomorrow and make sure you're all set up and have everything you need."

"That's very nice of him."

"Since he lives in the building, he's nearby. Feel free to call on him for anything. Even if you just need someone to talk to."

She nodded. "When are you leaving?"

"I have to leave now. Are you going to miss me?"

Staring into his indigo eyes, gazing at her with such warmth, took her breath away. She wanted to admit that she was falling deeply and hopelessly in love with him.

The elevator doors opened and the doorman exited with a cart full of her bags and packages. She drew herself up straight, thankful for the interruption.

"Take them into the master bedroom," Kane said to the doorman. Then he turned back to River. "I was wondering if those few bags you brought up with you were all you'd bought. I'm glad to see that you found so much more." He hooked his hand around her waist and pulled her close to his side. "So are you going to miss me?" he asked again.

"Of course," she said in a matter-of-fact manner. She was his wife. It's what she was supposed to say.

But she certainly didn't want to let him know it was true.

He was in this marriage to simplify his life. To have easy access to regular sex. And he'd chosen her because she had been a challenge . . . the one who'd gotten away.

With his looks and charm, he could have any woman he wanted, anytime, but she knew he worried about things like propriety and social expectations, so this is what worked for him.

But that meant she had to keep her heart on a tight leash. She couldn't let herself believe he might actually have feelings for her, other than basic affection.

And she could never admit to Kane how she really felt about him.

River sat on the couch, feeling very alone, wondering what to do next. Her nail polish supplies hadn't arrived yet, which was odd since Kane had said someone would bring them by. She'd already reviewed her promotion plans several times, and had started looking for more nail polish blogs online, but until she got her supplies, there wasn't much more she could do.

It hadn't even been twenty-four hours since Kane had left on his business trip and she'd never felt so alone or out of her element.

The phone rang—again—and she wished it would stop. Whoever it was could leave a message for Kane. The only ones who knew she was here were Kane and Will. Kane would call her on her cell and Will would just knock on the door, since he lived in the building.

She went into the kitchen and made herself dinner. Just a small salad, since there was little in the fridge. Tomorrow, she would have to get some groceries.

She put the TV on while she ate, then when she finished, placed the empty plate on the coffee table and slumped on the couch. It was weird being in this huge lavish place on her own. She certainly didn't look forward to sleeping in that big bed all alone again tonight. She had barely slept, the night filled with odd, unfamiliar noises.

Was this what it was going to be like being married to Kane? Bouts of great sex, sure, but then he'd disappear for days on end?

She walked to the kitchen and washed the few dishes, then decided she'd go in the hot tub. There was a private hot tub and a swimming pool in Kane's own private courtyard, separated by a glass wall between the living room and the spa room and another wall of glass to the pool. The sight of it had been calling to her all day. She walked into the room and gazed at the sunset beyond. The pool glimmered with the molten gold of the sky.

She grabbed one of the colorful beach towels from the shelf and searched around a bit, hoping she'd find a spare bathing suit, but no such luck. Hers had faded last summer and she'd tossed it out.

She bit her lip. It was totally private here, so there was no reason she couldn't just go in naked.

She found a hair clip and a covered elastic in the spa bathroom, so she gathered her hair into a ponytail and clipped it atop her head, then walked back into the spa room and glanced through the glass to the living room. Of course, there was no one there. She stripped down and set her clothes neatly on a lounge chair beside her towel, then walked to the sunken tub and settled into the hot water.

She glanced toward the living room again. Had she heard someone out there?

No, she'd been thrown off kilter all night because of noises she wasn't used to. No one was going to come in. She was all alone here.

She pushed the button to start the bubbles, then just settled back and closed her eyes. The hot water and the flow of the bubbles were so relaxing. She should have done this last night. Maybe then she would have slept better.

"River?"

Chapter Fourteen

River jolted forward at the male voice, her eyelids popping open. "What?"

Will stood in the doorway, looking concerned. "I've been calling all day and you didn't pick up."

"Oh." She started to stand and suddenly remembered she was totally naked. She wrapped her arm over her chest, but from the uncomfortable look on his face, he'd already seen more than she would have liked. Her cheeks flushed.

"You were the one calling?"

"Didn't Kane tell you I was going to stop by?" he asked.

"Yes, but I thought you'd just knock on the door."

"The elevator opens right into the penthouse, so there is no door. And I didn't want to just walk in on you."

"Oh, God, of course. I didn't even think of that. I'm sorry." She felt like an idiot, but she wasn't used to the idea of an elevator opening right into an apartment.

"It's okay. I just wanted to make sure you're okay. Now that I know you are, I'll just go."

"Wait. No." She knew she sounded a little desperate. "I'd really like some company."

At that moment, the bubbles turned off, leaving the water clear enough that she was totally visible. His gaze dropped to her body as she tried to cover herself, then veered away.

"I . . . uh . . . don't think that's a good idea," he said.

Oh, God, he thought she was coming on to him.

"No, I don't mean . . . I just thought maybe we could talk. I'm not used to being alone in this place and . . ." She bit her lip. "I'd really like some company. Maybe we could talk? Or watch a movie?"

"Okay, sure," he said, staring at the wall. "How about I order a pizza?"

She smiled, her stomach gurgling. "That would be nice." As he turned toward the door, she said, "Wait. Could you just hand me the towel on the chair there?"

He walked farther into the room and retrieved her towel, then walked toward the tub, his gaze averted. She took the towel from his outstretched hand, feeling very self-conscious at having him so close with her totally naked. But even if he'd gone back into the living room, the tub was visible through the glass wall, so she didn't want the towel that far away.

"I'll go call for the pizza." He walked across the room and went through the door.

As soon as she saw him disappear into the kitchen,

clearly trying to give her some privacy, she stood up and wrapped the towel securely around herself. She took a quick shower in the spa bathroom, then pulled on her clothes and brushed out her long hair.

She double-checked that all the buttons on her loose-fitting floral shirt were fastened, and then smoothed it down over her snug jeans. She left the bathroom and pushed open the glass door to the living room.

"The pizza will be here in a half hour." He sat in one of the armchairs beside the couch facing the TV. "What movie would you like to watch?"

"We could just talk until it gets here."

"Sure." He put down the remote control and sat back. "How are you settling in?"

She sank onto the couch. "Not very well. I'm not used to the place yet. I don't know where anything is and . . . well, that stove is so fancy I'm not quite sure how to make it work."

"Oh, yeah. Kane likes the latest technology. I'll show you how it works before I go."

She nodded then suddenly realized she was the hostess here. "Um, would you like a drink or something?"

"How about I get you something, since I know where everything is? We could open a bottle of wine to go with the pizza? Or would you like a beer?"

"Wine would be nice, thanks."

A few minutes later, he set a glass of red wine in front of her, and then sat down again.

"I'm sorry I didn't answer Kane's phone when you

called," she said. "I didn't think anyone would be calling for me."

"It's your phone now, too. And it wasn't just me. The doorman called when the grocery order arrived."

"Kane ordered groceries for me?"

Will laughed, a warm chuckle. "You don't think he'd leave you here with no food, do you?"

"No, I guess not."

He leaned back in the chair, stretching out his long legs. He was so different from Kane. Everything from his laid-back attitude to his casual clothes. Clearly, he was more at ease in the soft, faded denims designed for comfort and the band T-shirt he wore right now as opposed to Kane's casual look, which typically consisted of designer jeans that look like they were tailored to fit his body and crisp button-down shirts.

"So you must be pretty excited about your new nail polish launch," he said.

"Yeah, sure. I'm anxious to get started on making the polishes." She ran her palms over her denim-clad thighs. "I just hope they do okay. I'd hate to think Kane invested in me and pulled strings to get my line into Rapture, and then no one buys them."

"I'm sure that won't happen. Don't worry."

The anxiety about her line failing despite Kane's help had been building in her. A growing unease that was eating away at her. But Will's warm smile and the encouragement in his knowing hazel eyes soothed her agitation. Maybe she had been blowing things out of proportion.

She drew in a deep breath. "I know. I'll just do the best I can. That's all I can expect of myself. It's just, it's been my dream, you know?"

He nodded. "I do. I didn't come from money like Kane did. When I met him at college and he was impressed by my ideas then said he wanted to start a business together, I knew my dream had come true."

She gazed at him, realizing for the first time how much they had in common.

"I think it's amazing that you two paired up and have become such a phenomenal success. Your company is practically a household name."

"I was definitely lucky. Kane is a fabulous friend and business partner." He smiled. "And I know he'll be a fabulous husband."

Of course he was right. Kane would be everything a husband should be. Strong, protective, understanding. A good provider. He would meet her every need.

Except one.

He would never love her.

"So now that you've had your dream become a reality, do you have other dreams?" she asked.

"Well, I don't need any more money. And that's never been important to me anyway. I've always just wanted to be able to bring my ideas to life. But . . . I guess the big thing I want in life is to find that special person. You know, someone who puts me above all else. Who loves me."

Her heart ached. She wanted that, too, but now she was in a marriage of convenience, so she would never have it.

But she smiled. "You're a romantic."

He nodded. "I guess I am. And I want the whole white picket fence thing. I want to get a house like you and Kane have and fill it with kids."

"I'm sure you'll have all of that," she said softly. "It'll just take a little time to find that special someone."

He stared at the wineglass in his hand. "I thought I had, but it didn't work out."

At the sadness she saw in his eyes, her heart ached for him.

She rested her hand on his. "I'm sorry, Will. It must hurt."

He shrugged. "Life moves on."

The feel of River's soft hand on his threw Will totally off balance. She seemed to sense his discomfort and drew her hand away, then sipped her wine.

What the hell was he doing moaning about his own life when he was here to cheer River up?

She set her glass on the table and leaned back against the couch. She looked so morose. Well, why wouldn't she? She'd been uprooted from her life and thrown into a totally new situation.

She'd been fired from her job, married a man she didn't love, and then moved out of her apartment into this new place. It was luxurious, but that didn't make it home. Not yet.

She was starting a new company, which was in a great position because of Kane's backing, but she had the same worries as every new business owner. That her product wouldn't be well received and her dream would all fall apart around her.

With Kane out of town for a week, she didn't even have her husband to talk through her anxiety with.

Kane had asked Will to check on her while he was gone. Will had a key card that allowed him access to the penthouse, but he wouldn't just walk in on Kane's new bride.

Except that he'd started to get worried when she hadn't answered his repeated calls today.

Then to find her naked in the hot tub . . .

Fuck! He would never make a move on a woman Kane was interested in, let alone his new wife, but seeing her all sexy and soft-looking in the water had made him hard and needy. With his own sex life a nonevent right now, it had been hard to ignore the soft swell of her breasts being caressed by the bubbling water. And knowing that only the thin veil of water and air had been hiding the rest of her assets.

When the bubbles had turned off, exposing all of her . . . Fuck! He shifted uncomfortably in the chair, the mere memory of it making him hard again. She'd moved her arm over her breasts and slid a hand over her lower region, but not before he'd gotten an eyeful.

If he was smart, he'd hightail it out of here right now . . . but she so clearly needed someone to talk to.

"You've known Kane a long time," she said. "You must be really close friends."

"That's right. I'd do anything for Kane."

"How much do you know about why he married me?"

"I don't really want to talk about that. It's really between the two of you."

She nodded. "I just wondered if you thought it was strange."

"Kane does things in his own way. And he always gets what he wants. I've learned not to question his methods."

"He cares so much about what people think. I assume he wants the appearance of propriety being married gives him."

"You don't think he married you out of love?"

She glanced at him. "I thought Kane said you knew. I . . ." Then she bit her lip as if she'd done something wrong.

He knew that she wasn't supposed to tell anyone about the reason they got married, so she must be afraid she'd violated that stipulation.

"I know you married him because of a business deal."

He didn't want to say more. He knew Kane wanted her more than he'd ever wanted anyone before and when she'd refused to give their relationship a second chance, Kane had used the deal to pressure her into marrying him. He also knew Kane was a little confused about his own feelings, especially since they were all tied up with the guilt he felt about what had happened in college. But he also knew Kane didn't need love to be part of marriage. He was very practical and had told Will—many times—how good the sex was between him and River.

That, and the fact his desire for her had never diminished after all these years, was enough for him.

But Will wasn't confused. He knew that Kane loved her, even if Kane hadn't figured it out himself.

"I can't help wondering what you think of me," River said.

He smiled. "I think you're a very practical young woman who makes my friend very happy."

The pizza arrived. He brought out plates and served her a slice, then sat down beside her.

She took a bite. "It's really good."

They both sipped wine and ate their dinner. When they were done, he told himself he should leave. Now.

But she still looked so sad.

Her eyes seemed to shimmer. "Thank you for staying with me. I feel a bit overwhelmed with being here alone, and all the changes."

"I get it. It's a lot to process."

She shook her head. "You don't understand. I feel so alone. I don't feel like I belong here. Everything has changed and I . . ." Her voice cracked and tears welled in her eyes.

He wrapped his arm around her and pulled her against his side. She rested her head on his shoulder and settled against him. God, it just felt too . . . good.

He picked up the remote control. "Want to watch a movie now?"

"Sure. Anything you like."

He turned something on—one of the latest on The

Movie Channel—and barely noticed what was happening on the screen. He was too aware of River snuggled close beside him.

But he was loath to let her go, since she was obviously still hurting.

River couldn't believe she was snuggled up to Kane's best friend. Not that anything would happen between them. Of course it wouldn't. But it felt so good being next to him, his protective arm around her.

And she was so tired. She'd barely slept at all last night and she was sleepy.

The movie droned on and she found her eyelids closing. She snuggled closer and soon fell fast asleep.

When she woke up, it was dark and a blanket was tossed over her. She lifted her head and glanced around. Will was nowhere to be seen.

Then she saw the note on the coffee table.

Call me anytime.

Then his phone number below.

She sighed and glanced at the clock. It was two a.m. And she was alone again.

She pushed herself up from the couch and wandered to the bedroom, then climbed into the bed. But instead of falling asleep, she tossed and turned for hours. Finally, she got up and went into the den and sat at the desk in front of Kane's desktop computer.

She'd tried to connect to the Internet on her laptop earlier in the day, but she didn't know the WiFi password, and she didn't think Kane would mind if she used his computer to read her e-mail. She clicked on the mail icon and scanned the few e-mails there. Mostly notifications of new posts on nail polish blogs she followed. She opened a video tutorial by her favorite blogger and watched a new water-marbling technique. The woman used several shades of a new metallic collection and the result was shiny swirls of perfection. River closed her e-mail, but wasn't ready to go back to bed yet, so she decided to watch a movie.

She found a movie viewer in his list of apps and opened it. Maybe he had a selection.

She opened the last one viewed and was immediately taken aback. What she saw on the screen was Kane, sitting back in . . . she glanced around . . . yes, in this chair and he was obviously getting a blow job. The top of a woman's head was barely visible as it bobbed in and out of view, but the camera was focused on Kane's broad, naked chest and face. His head was back and sheer pleasure glowed from him.

River watched in awe, her insides heating at the sight of her husband being pleasured by another woman. She felt a bit jealous, but knew that was crazy. This video had been taken before they were married. She knew she should turn it off, but she was mesmerized. Seeing the delight on his face . . . imagining his cock was buried in her own mouth as she gave him such joy . . . sent hormones surging through her.

He moaned and his features tightened. River felt her own ache building, and her fingers glided inside her pajamas and found her slickness. She stroked herself as the woman's head moved faster. She flicked over her clit as Kane's fingers glided over the woman's short hair and guided her head forward and back.

Oh, God, this was so sexy watching him. She arched against her hand as he groaned, clearly coming. She flicked faster, feeling her own release near at hand. She pushed her fingers inside her wet opening and pumped, then stroked her clit again.

Just as she found her release, the person on her knees stood up and . . .

Oh, God, it wasn't a woman at all.

It was Will.

Chapter Fifteen

River woke up to the sound of her cell phone ring tone. She grabbed it from the nightstand.

"Hello?" Her voice was hoarse and she cleared her throat.

"Hi. It's Kane. Everything okay?"

She pushed herself up. "Yeah, of course. Why?"

He couldn't have known she'd seen the video.

"Will called me yesterday and left a message saying he couldn't get ahold of you all day. I was tied up until late last night and didn't check my messages until just now."

She pushed her hair back from her face. "I just wasn't picking up the landline. I figured the calls would be for you and they'd leave a message. Stupid, I know. Will did come over though. He stayed for pizza and we watched a movie."

"Good. He's my best friend, so I'm glad to know you're getting a chance to bond."

"Yeah, I can tell you two are really close." Oh, God, why had she said that?

But she knew exactly why she'd said it. Because she was resentful that he'd withheld the truth from her, and a little worried that Kane was having sex with Will while they were married.

That maybe that's why Kane had *really* married her. To hide his relationship with Will. Kane cared too much about what other people thought to be comfortable with anyone knowing he was in love with another man.

"Are you sure everything's okay? You sound a bit off."

"No, I'm fine. It's just a little strange being here on my own. I'm not used to it yet."

"I'm sorry. I hated leaving you so soon, but it couldn't be helped. I'll be back in a few days. And you know . . ." there was a definite smile in his voice, "if you're feeling lonely, we could talk for a while now. You're in bed, right?"

"Yes, of course." It was seven in the morning.

"So am I," he said seductively.

Oh, God. He wanted to have phone sex. And since sex was part of their agreement, if that's what he wanted . . .

"I . . . uh . . . yeah. I'm naked and . . . uh . . . I'm wanting you." The words sounded so stiff, but she couldn't help it.

He laughed. "Okay, I get it. You're not in the mood."

"No, I just . . . I mean, I've never . . ."

"It's all right. I can wait until I get back and we see each other in person. I look forward to stripping off all your clothes . . . piece by piece . . . revealing your naked, sexy body and kissing you everywhere. Especially your hot, wet pussy. Licking it and stroking until you're panting for air. Then making you come until you scream out my name."

Oh, God, she was in the mood now.

"That would be"—she gulped—"nice." She ran her hand over her breast. "Maybe we could try again now."

He chuckled. "Sorry. Too late now," he said in a teasing voice.

"But—"

"I'll call you later." Then he ended the call.

River finally fell back asleep for a while, and then got up around eight-thirty. She pulled up her spreadsheet and reviewed the cost of the supplies she'd ordered and checked the cost per bottle against the various price points she'd been considering. She'd done this all before, but until she actually received the supplies, there was little she could do to make progress.

She finally decided to go out for a swim in the pool—this time in a bra and panties covered with a T-shirt. Just in case.

She ate some cereal for breakfast, since she hadn't gotten the groceries from Will yet. She showered and dressed, then called Will.

"Hi. It's River. I was hoping I could come by and pick up the groceries," she said when he answered.

"I can bring them over right now, if you like," he said. "I've also got your nail polish supplies. They were delivered yesterday, too."

"I don't want to take you away from work," she said.

"Not at all. I was going to help you get set up today."

A few minutes later, he arrived with the boxes. He set them on the kitchen table, and then moved the box of food to the kitchen counter. She felt very awkward being around him after seeing him in that video. Knowing he and her husband had been lovers.

And maybe still were.

"How are you this morning?" he asked with a smile.

"Oh, fine." She started unpacking the groceries, laying the vegetables and packages of meat on the counter.

Will put them in the fridge while she grabbed some cans from the box. Although the kitchen was large, she kept coming into contact with him. A brush of his arm as he reached for a bag of flour from the box, her hip bumping his when she turned around after putting the milk in the fridge. Then her butt backed into his crotch as she was putting onions under the counter and he reached over her to put away a box of cereal.

She stood up and tugged on the hem of her T-shirt, then returned to the box. It was empty now. Will took it off the counter. River grabbed some scissors from the drawer and walked to the table, then opened the big box that held her nail polish supplies.

She stared at various bottles of base, pigments, glitters, and flakies inside with a smile of delight. There were also nail polish bottles, steel mixing balls, and she'd bought extra funnels and measuring spoons. She already had labels, and had ordered some small black boxes to place each bottle in to give the packaging a higher-end feel.

Will laughed. "I hope you look at Kane with that same look of awe."

She started pulling the bottles out of the box. Will didn't say anything when she didn't answer, but he must be feeling the awkwardness. Which wasn't fair of her. He was giving up his valuable time to help her and . . . well, she knew this wasn't a real marriage to Kane. If Kane was keeping a lover, even one that she had to see all the time, that was his prerogative. He hadn't told her about it—and there was no reason he had to—and she wondered if that was exactly so she wouldn't feel awkward around Will.

Will helped her unpack all the items and organize them on the table.

She picked up a couple of little baggies of glitter, admiring the lovely colors.

"Where are we going to work?" Will asked.

We. It felt so strange to her that this wealthy business entrepreneur, a partner in a big corporation, was going to spend the day helping her mix nail polish.

"I guess on the kitchen counter. I'll lay some plastic down to protect the granite countertop."

"Wait, it says on this bottle," he said, reading the label of the suspension base, "that you need to work in a well-ventilated area."

"Sure, I'll turn on the fan and open the window."

"I don't think we should chance that. It's a nice day out. Why don't we work out by the pool?"

Her automatic reaction was to resist his suggestion. But he was right. She needed to be careful about breathing in the chemicals and pigments. Fighting him would just be spiting herself. She agreed and selected the base, pigments, and glitters she'd be using today and put them back in the box, then tossed in the mixing utensils and bottles. He carried them outside.

He set out the opened polish bottles and she used a syringe to draw the base from the big bottle and fill ten of the little bottles, then she popped a little funnel in each and measured out pigment and dropped it in the funnels.

"Are you really going to do this a bottle at a time?" Will asked.

"Well, for now. I've never done a bulk set of polish before. I'm afraid if I mix it in a bigger bottle, it might not come out right."

She handed him a toothpick. "You can push the pigment down. It tends to clump in the funnel."

Will sat and poked the powder with the sharp wooden pick to loosen it while she measured some of the silver holo glitter and tossed it in on top, and then she added some fine peacock-blue glitter.

When they had all ten bottles done, she used her little hand-held mixer to blend everything, then Will dropped two steel balls in each and capped them. Finally, ten complete bottles sat on the table, glistening in the sunlight. She smiled, ridiculously happy that she had just made the first step in her growing business.

"Now just three hundred and ninety to go," Will said.

"Actually, we still have another fifty or so over that to

do," she said as she assembled one of the flattened, divided boxes she'd bought to store the polish. "I plan to send several sets out to bloggers and YouTube vloggers for review." She placed the full bottles inside.

Then she glanced his way, wondering if he would abandon her now that he'd gotten her started.

"Okay, well, we'd better get moving then." He started setting out more of the small glass bottles.

Will enjoyed working with River. Her obvious joy at working with these colors and bright glitters made him smile. She seemed to genuinely appreciate his help, too, but he sensed something was off. Last night, they had gotten to know each other a little better and seemed to be forming a bond, but today she seemed tense around him. Whenever he got too close, like when they were putting away the groceries or when he accidentally brushed her arm when he was setting out the little bottles, she stiffened.

They spent the whole day filling bottles and mixing polish. She did a batch of several different colors and he loved watching the delight in her eyes when she opened a new colorant or glitter pouch.

Finally, when she showed no signs of stopping, Will leaned back in his chair and sighed.

"Time for a break. How about some dinner?"

"Oh, no, I don't want to take up any more of your time."

He was sure she was trying to get rid of him, but he was intent on finding out what had gone wrong between them.

"I insist. You've got some steaks in there. How about I show you how to use the grill on the stove?"

"Okay. Thanks," she said reluctantly. She placed the latest box of finished polish on the growing stack, and then followed Will into the house.

Will showed her the various controls on the stove, and he spiced up the steaks while she made a salad. Soon they were sitting at the table with dinner and a nice red wine. When they were finished, he sat back and watched her sip her wine.

"So I notice you've been a bit uncomfortable around me today. Did I do something wrong last night?"

She gazed at her wine as she swirled it in her glass. "No. It was very nice of you to keep me company yesterday."

"Okay, if it's not that, then what's wrong?"

She shook her head. "There's nothing wrong."

"I don't believe you. Look, I'm Kane's best friend . . . you're his wife . . . I'd like us to be friends. If I've done anything wrong, I'd like a chance to fix it."

"You didn't do anything wrong. It's just . . . an awkward situation."

"What is? The reason you and Kane are married?"

She pursed her lips. "The fact that I'm married to Kane, but that you two are . . . uh . . ." She shrugged.

"Partners? I'm not sure how that's awkward."

"No, I mean . . ." She gazed his way, and bit her lip. "I know that you and Kane . . . that you're . . . more than just business partners."

His stomach clenched. "You mean friends?" But he was sure that wasn't it.

She shook her head.

"What do you mean, River?"

"I mean that you two are . . . lovers."

He sighed and sat back in the chair. How the hell did she know?

"Did Kane tell you?" he asked.

Kane had told Will that he didn't want her to know. That it would make things awkward between all of them.

"No, he didn't say a thing. I . . . well, it was an accident, but . . . I found a video on Kane's computer." She gazed at him with wide eyes. "I wasn't snooping. I just wanted to watch a movie and . . ."

"It's okay. I don't think that. I . . . Ah, fuck, River. We didn't want you to know. We didn't want it to be awkward for you."

She nodded and sipped more of her wine. "It's just strange. The idea that he's having sex with me and that you two are still . . ." She trailed off.

"What? No. We aren't still together like that." He reached across the table and took her hand. "When he told me he was going after you again, he ended it with me. You are his full focus. He is totally and completely dedicated to making things work between you."

River stared at Will, the warmth of his hand surrounding hers comforting.

"Really?" she asked, elated.

"Of course. He will be totally faithful to you."

"I . . ." But she choked up. She sipped her wine again and cleared her throat. "But what about you? Do you still love him?"

"I want him to be happy. And our friendship will always be sound. I think the only thing that could threaten that is if you decide you don't want me around."

Her heart ached as he said the words. "You really think he'd shut you out of his life if I didn't like you?"

Will nodded. "His personal life, yes. If it made you uncomfortable. We'd still run the business together, but he might go so far as to ask me to relocate. Then we'd run business meetings over Skype."

She couldn't believe she'd have so much power over Kane's life.

She squeezed Will's hand. "Don't worry. I'm not going to do anything to jeopardize your friendship with Kane. I promise."

After their conversation, River felt more relaxed around Will.

He was a good friend to Kane. She couldn't believe that he would put his friend's happiness ahead of his own that way. But then, people did that kind of thing for the people they love.

Was Will in love with Kane? The thought broke River's heart. That he was in love with Kane and couldn't be with him.

If she hadn't accepted this business proposal with

Kane . . . to be his wife in return for building her business . . . would he have stayed with Will?

But she knew in her heart that Kane would never be willing to make his relationship with Will public. Kane would want a marriage that his friends and family would find acceptable, and that was her role.

She and Will cleared the table, and then they did the dishes together. After that, they settled into the living room with another bottle of wine. Will popped the cork and filled her glass.

Will was a good-looking man. Sexy and charismatic. And she felt safe and comfortable around him. She was sure they could become good friends. And she was amazed that he didn't resent her. Or if he did, he hid it well.

They chatted and laughed. And drank more wine.

"I love how engaged you are when you're mixing your nail polish," he said. "You so clearly love it." He smiled. "And you're very talented."

She shrugged off the compliment. "As you saw, there's no real magic. I just mix the ingredients together."

"I'm not letting you get away with that. It's your unique creativity that allows you to combine everything just so to make something beautiful."

Elation filled her at his encouragement.

She rested her head against his shoulder. "That's nice of you to say."

He slid his arm around her. She was sure he sensed that she didn't get much encouragement. Of course, he knew how people had viewed her in college. They didn't call her creative. They just called her strange.

She gazed at his beautiful hazel eyes, so thoughtful and full of warmth. A tingling started deep inside her, followed by a coiling heat.

"What are you thinking?" he asked.

She giggled. "To tell the truth, I was thinking that it's a good thing you're gay."

He frowned. "Why? Because that makes me safe to be around?"

"No. Because you're so attractive and I'm a married woman." She giggled again. Oh, God, had she really said that out loud?

He tucked his finger under her chin and tipped it up, his expressive eyes heating.

"River, get this straight. I am not gay."

Then his lips found hers and she sucked in a breath. Then leaned into the kiss.

His mouth moved gently on hers, and then his tongue slipped between her lips. Her arms glided around him without her consent and she held him close. Their mouths moved together and heat spiraled through her.

Then he ended the kiss. "Fuck, I didn't mean to do that."

"Then why the hell did you?"

River's gaze darted across the room to see Kane standing there glaring at them.

Chapter Sixteen

River's chest constricted. "Kane . . ."

Will was on his feet. "Man, I'm sorry. But nothing happened."

"It didn't look like nothing to me. To *me* it looked like you were hitting on my wife."

"Kane, you know I'd never do that."

"I'd believe that a lot more if I hadn't just seen you manhandling her."

River had never seen Kane so angry. It was palpable, like an electrical field crackling around him.

"Now get the fuck out of here."

Will frowned and sent her a glance, then strode across the room. A moment later, she heard the doors of the elevator close behind him.

She drew in a breath as the silence hung around them. Kane's indigo eyes turned to her, and she shifted under his angry stare.

"Kane, it wasn't Will's fault. It just—"

"Stop," he snapped, his eyes blazing. "And you're right. It wasn't his fault. You're my wife and you have certain responsibilities. That includes not letting another man touch you."

She watched him, forlorn, and more than a little un-nerved by the anger blazing from him.

"And there's another responsibility you have as my wife." He unfastened his belt and pulled it from his pants. She tensed, for a split second, afraid he intended to hit her with it.

But she realized the blind fear was just a flash from her past. Kane was not her father. He was nothing like him. Kane would never hurt her like that.

He tossed the belt aside as he walked purposely toward her. He grabbed her hand and pulled her to her feet. Their gazes locked and the disappointment and . . . oh, God, the pain—deep and poignant—in his eyes, took her breath away.

He placed his hand on top of her head and pushed her down, until she was on her knees. He unzipped his pants and pulled out his cock. It was long and flaccid.

"You know what to do."

She wrapped her hand around it and immediately it began to stiffen.

This was so strange, kneeling in front of him, anger still emanating from him. But she knew no amount of talking would fix what had happened, and she had no idea what she would say anyway.

Kane's eyes closed as River's hand stroked his cock. His heart pounded as the blinding pain of Will's betrayal—and hers—continued to pulse through him, but her fingers around his cock transformed the pain into something else. Her hand glided his length, his cock growing within her grip. Need pulsed through him. To be in her mouth.

"Suck it," he growled.

Immediately, she took him between her lips. He almost groaned at the feel of his cockhead fully immersed in the warmth of her mouth. He just wanted to forget what he'd seen. To lose himself in these new sensations.

He coiled his hand in her hair and drew her forward, filling her. Need pulsed through him at the feel of her heat totally surrounding him.

Then he let her draw back again.

"Faster," he commanded.

She responded by increasing the rhythm. Her hand found his balls and she stroked as her mouth took him again and again.

He was getting close. In moments, he would spew inside her.

But he didn't want that. He tugged her head back, and pulled her to her feet.

"Strip."

She looked at him hesitantly, but at his hard gaze, she started unbuttoning her top. It was too slow. He grabbed the sides of the shirt and ripped it open, her buttons scattering, then pushed it down her shoulders. She let it drop to the floor, then quickly unfastened her jeans and pushed them down.

"All of it," he demanded as she stood in her purple bra and panties, gazing at him uncertainly.

She shed the feminine scraps of lace and now stood before him naked. His heart pounded and his cock ached to be inside her.

He dropped his pants and boxers, never tearing his gaze from her. Her nipples were puckered and hard. Her exposed pussy set him on fire. He needed to drive his aching cock into her right now.

To claim her as his own.

He dragged her to him and took her mouth, thrusting his tongue inside, backing her up to the wall. But he could imagine he tasted Will on her lips and that sent a new surge of rage through him. When he released her mouth, he couldn't stand looking at her, knowing she had betrayed him, so he spun her around, pushing her hard against the wall, then glided his hard, aching cock between her thighs.

Fuck, her slickness glazed his shaft.

But was it for him, or because of Will?

Kane's big body held River tight to the wall, her breasts crushed against the cool surface, her cheek hard against it. The feel of his cock gliding over her wet slit made her heart pump faster.

Oh, God, she wanted him inside her. Even as angry

as he was. He pressed his cockhead to her opening, and then drove into her. Hard.

She gasped. His body crushed her against the wall, and then he drew back.

Then he surged forward again.

Her insides vibrated with need.

He drew back and thrust again. Then again.

He took her fast and hard, his powerful shaft pounding into her over and over.

Wild, primal pleasure surged through her. Pulsing through her veins like liquid fire.

His mouth found her neck and he nipped, making her gasp.

Then he erupted inside her, groaning. The fountain of heat within her depths threw her over the edge. She wailed her release as he kept driving into her.

She was still trapped against the wall by his big body. She could feel his heart thumping against her.

It felt like they stood there forever, their bodies joined. Their heartbeats in sync.

Finally, he pulled away. His cock slid from inside her and she ached at the emptiness.

Then he just walked away. She heard a door close. When she finally pushed herself from the wall, her knees were rubbery. She picked up her clothes and pulled them on, then picked up his discarded pants and folded them, then set them on the chair.

Oh, God, she didn't want to think about the repercussions of that one kiss between her and Will. She didn't even understand how it had happened, but now she was afraid that Kane and Will would lose even more than they already had.

Would Kane end their friendship for good?

And as much as she cared about that, her heart ached even more for herself, because she knew that she would never be more to Kane than his fake wife, there for sexual release and societal propriety. He would never actually love her.

Which was all the worse because, deep inside, she knew she was in love with him.

River went out to the pool and retrieved the boxes of polish she and Will had left there. It was getting dark out now. It took a couple of trips to bring them in and she set them on a shelf Kane had cleared away for that purpose in the big walk-in closet in the hallway. She cleared the dishes and tidied up, ensuring the wine bottle was out of sight in the recycle bin, and generally making sure there was no sign that Will had been here.

She glanced around, unsure what to do now. She didn't want to sit in the living room on her own, knowing Kane might just reappear, wanting to talk. She just couldn't face that right now. And she couldn't face climbing into bed with him.

So she went to the guest room and undressed, then climbed into bed. When she woke up in the morning, Kane was gone again. The master bedroom door was open and she saw his suitcase laying open on the love seat by the fireplace. She hung up his suits and put his other clothes in the hamper, then put the suitcase away.

She spent the day making more nail polish, but ensured everything was cleaned up by five o'clock, and then started making dinner. She just made a simple chicken casserole. She didn't know how to make the fancy food he was probably used to, but it was her best recipe.

When he finally arrived, she glanced at him nervously, but he just disappeared into the bedroom and changed. When he returned in nice jeans and a sage-green casual shirt, he looked heart-meltingly handsome.

"I was going to suggest we eat out," he said casually, "but I take it you've made something for dinner."

The aroma of the chicken wafted from the kitchen.

"It's just a casserole. Nothing fancy."

"It'll be fine."

When she served dinner, he ate a good portion and commended her on it, but mostly they hardly spoke. Afterward, when she cleared away the dishes, he sat in the living room and turned his focus to his tablet, probably reading the news.

She wasn't really sure what to do with herself, still not used to being in this place. Will had shown her how to access the WiFi, so she opened her laptop and put headphones on and watched a movie on Netflix.

"River?"

She dragged her gaze from the movie, which was nearing the end, to see Kane standing before her.

"I'm going to bed."

She gazed at him, not sure what he wanted her to say.

"Let's get this straight," he continued. "You'll be sleeping in the master bedroom with me tonight." He held out his hand to her.

"The movie's almost over," she hazarded.

"You can finish it tomorrow."

She drew in a breath and shut down the app, then closed her laptop. As Kane's hand closed around hers and he led her to the bedroom, her heart started to pound.

Even though their marriage wasn't the real thing, the short time he'd been gone had seemed interminable, and the angry sex they'd shared yesterday had left her wanting . . . needing . . . to feel some closeness with him.

Once in the bedroom, he turned to her, then slowly and purposefully stripped away her top and jeans. While she stood in her bra and panties, he stripped off his own clothes, and then lay down on the bed. He wrapped his hand around his semi-erect cock and watched her.

"Take off the rest for me."

She watched his hand glide the length of his shaft as she reached behind herself and released the hooks on her bra, and then slowly eased the straps off her shoulders and down her arms. His cock grew harder under his stroking hand, now a tall tower of rigid flesh. She dropped her bra to the floor, watching his indigo eyes darken.

Then she pushed down her panties. Now totally naked, she walked toward the bed. He released his erection and held out his hand. When she took it, he drew her onto the bed and over him.

She ached for him, wanting the big cock inside her. She settled her body over him and grasped his hot, hard flesh, then guided it to her slick opening.

He hadn't even touched her and she was wet with need. She lowered herself, his thick shaft stretching her as it filled her up. She couldn't help moaning as she glided down his hard erection.

She sat staring at him, their gazes locked.

"Fuck me, sweetheart. Make me come," he said.

Oh, God, his words . . . the heat in his eyes . . .

She was burning up with need. She started to move on him, the feel of his thick cockhead stroking her insides overwhelming. She squeezed him, groaning at the intense pleasure.

"Show me how much you want me," he murmured.

She rose and fell faster, his cock gliding within her.

She did want him. She *needed* him. Deep inside her. Surging into her body.

Making her tremble.

She bounced up and down, taking him deeper and faster. His breathing quickened and his eyes blazed with a reflection of her own need.

"Oh, God, I'm going to come," she blurted, the sweet joy coiling inside her, suddenly swelling.

"Yes, sweetheart. Do it. Come for me."

His hands grasped her hips and guided her faster. Joyful sensations skittered along her nerve endings and she sucked in a breath, then pleasure burst through her in an explosion of ecstasy. He groaned and she could feel him erupt inside her.

Finally, she collapsed against him. As soon as she caught her breath, she tried to shift to the side, the feel of her breasts against his hot, hard chest too much for her. But his arm tightened around her waist and she couldn't move away.

After a moment, he pressed one hand to the small of her back and rolled onto his side, keeping her in his firm grasp, and turned out the bedside light. They lay in the darkness, her body tight to his . . . and his cock still buried inside her. In fact, it was still hard.

She lay in the dark, lulled by his closeness, resisting the urge to squeeze him inside her. But he lay silently and after a while she dozed off.

River awoke to a heady heat, feeling his big cock moving inside her. Just slow, short strokes at first. She murmured and her arms slid around him. He nuzzled her neck and his hard flesh glided deeper. His strokes became longer. She moaned softly as her most sensitive flesh quivered at the steady invasion.

He rolled her onto her back and glided deeper still. She opened her legs wider, wrapping them around his waist, welcoming him inside. He groaned and thrust harder. The pace picked up speed, as did her breathing.

"Oh, it feels so good," she murmured against his ear.

He moaned and thrust, hard and fast now. She gasped as he drilled deep into her.

"Yes. Please." She pulled him tighter to her body. "More."

He nipped her ear and she gasped again. "Come for me. I need to hear you come."

His cock filled her again and again.

"Yes, I . . ." She hung on to him tightly as her body quivered with building anticipation. The pleasure swelled and . . . "Oh, Kane." She gasped as she felt the pleasure consuming her. Then she catapulted over the edge. "I'm coming. Yesss." She wailed her release, clinging to his shoulders as she shot into freefall.

She was barely aware of his body pounding against hers, and then he groaned, his hips grinding against her. Still moaning, she continued riding the wave of ecstasy, his cock continuing to fill her with pleasure.

Finally, his movements slowed and she sucked in air as she settled back to earth. He held her tightly, and rolled her back with him. She faded into sleep again in the warmth of his arms.

River felt a soft brush of lips against her cheek and murmured softly, barely awake. A moment later, she heard the soft bump of the bedroom door closing, and she realized that Kane's strong arms were no longer around her, and the comfort of his warm solid body pressed to hers was gone.

Last night, they'd been so close and passionate. Intimate in a more emotional way somehow.

Vaguely the numbers on the clock—7:20—flashed in her brain before she dozed off again. Then her eyelids fluttered open and she glanced at the clock. It was 8:10. Kane would be leaving for the office soon. If he hadn't already.

She wanted to see him before he left. It became an overwhelming need and she pushed aside the covers and grabbed her silk robe, then raced from the room. She hurried down the hall and didn't see him in the living room or dining room. His briefcase wasn't visible.

She hurried into the kitchen, and stopped when she saw him sitting at the table by the window, reading his tablet, his finger flicking across the screen. The memory of those fingers lingering over her body last night sent tremors through her.

She walked toward him and he glanced her way.

"Good morning," he said. "I tried not to wake you."

She didn't answer, but reached for his tablet and took it from his hands and set it on the table. Then she slid in front of him, sitting on his lap, facing him. Her robe, which she'd barely taken time to tie, loosened and when he slid his arms around her, one glided under the robe around her waist. The feel of his fingers on her naked skin caused her nerve endings to spark in excitement. She captured his lips in a soft, gentle kiss, and then deepened it. His hand glided down her spine and flattened on her lower back and he drew her closer. Her insides melted with need. She wanted him inside her so badly.

"Kane, please forgive me for what happened." She stared into his indigo eyes, seeking some sign of forgiveness. She stroked his cheek, freshly shaved and smooth. "I don't ever want to hurt you, and I would never want to do anything to endanger our marriage."

Chapter Seventeen

When Kane's eyes glowed with warmth and he smiled, River desperately bit back the rest of what she wanted to blurt out.

That she loved him. Heart and soul.

That she never wanted to lose him.

But she couldn't tell him that. Not without ruining everything, since that wasn't what he wanted from this marriage.

"It's all right, baby. We're fine."

He kissed her, and the gentle movement of his lips on hers . . . the feel of his hand gliding along her spine . . . tightened the yearning inside her. The slippery fabric of the robe fell from her shoulder to her elbow. She started to shrug the other side down, too, but a soft rumble of laughter sounded deep in his chest and he leaned back, his gaze falling to her exposed breasts. Heat simmered through her and she wanted to feel his hands on her. Stroking her aching nipples. Cupping her in his large hands. But he eased the robe back up and pulled the front together, then tied the sash securely.

"Don't look so rejected," he said, his eyes glittering. "I'd love nothing more than to carry you back to bed and make passionate love to you." He stroked her hair behind her ear. Tingles danced along her neck. "But I intend to wait until we can do it slowly and leisurely." He smiled. "And I definitely like the idea of you thinking about me all day. Wanting me. Anticipating the next time we're together."

Her heart stuttered at the thought of him walking in the door this evening and sweeping her into his arms then into his bed, stripping away everything she wore until she was naked and vulnerable beneath him. She could imagine the gentle pressure of his hands on her skin . . . the nudge of his cockhead against her slick opening . . . the feel of him gliding inside.

"And I don't want you to think that all I want from you is sex." He stroked her cheek, and glided his fingers through her hair, his indigo eyes growing somber. "Especially after what I said the other night. I want you to know that you are more to me than just a sexual partner."

He drew her into another kiss and his mouth moved on hers with passion. She melted against him, her heart swelling.

Could he mean . . . ? Dare she hope he actually had feelings for her?

River walked into Giselle's and glanced around. Tia was with a customer, so River walked to the jewelry counter, checking out the newest arrivals. There were some lovely chains and a large, star-shaped crystal pendant that glittered rose, purple, and green, depending on the angle of the light, caught her eye.

"Hi. May I help you with anything?"

River glanced around at the sound of Tia's voice.

Tia's eyes lit up. "My God, look at you! I didn't even recognize you."

River wore the same green dress she'd had on the day she came home after selecting a new wardrobe with Kane's personal shopper. She loved this dress and especially loved the way Kane's eyes had heated when he'd first seen her in it. That's why she'd worn it today. To feel closer to Kane.

"You've changed. You look so much more sophisticated."

River frowned. "I'm not sure I like that."

Tia laughed. "No, it's a good thing. You're evolving. Finding a new style. But whatever look you wind up with will always be your own."

But would it be?

"You still have five minutes before you can leave for lunch, right? So help me find a scarf to add some pizzazz to my outfit." River lifted the star pendant from the display. "Maybe start with these colors."

Half an hour later, she sat across from Tia at the restaurant, setting the bags with her new purchases on the bench seat beside her in the booth. After leaving Giselle's, they'd seen a stunning pair of shoes in the window of the high-end shoe store a few doors down, a place she and Tia had only dreamed of shopping in. The shoes had slender heels that went on forever and were covered with tiny beads, forming a mosaic of colors . . . primarily the same as those in the scarf and pendant. Tia had insisted she go in and try them on and River instantly fell in love with them.

"I really think I can make a nail polish that will color shift like the pendant," River said as the waitress filled their glasses with water.

"I'm sure you can. And you're probably planning a caviar mani to go with the shoes. I bet you already have beads in the right colors."

"You're right." River couldn't help grinning broadly.

It was so nice being around Tia again. With Tia, River felt open about her creativity. And encouraged. Tia always spurred her to go further, rather than draw back like Kane did.

"So how's married life?" Tia asked.

"It's different, you know. It takes some getting used to."

"But you love the guy?" Tia asked with eyebrow raised.

River locked gazes with Tia, seeing the concern in her friend's sky-blue eyes.

"I do," River said with certainty.

She didn't mention that Kane didn't love her back.

This morning when he'd said she meant more to him than just a sexual partner, she'd started to hope . . . But once he left for work and her saner mind returned, she realized he'd meant he liked her and wanted them to have more between them than just sex. He hadn't meant he loved her.

Tia smiled and squeezed her hand. "You know, this time I believe you. And I think this marriage will be good for you."

Maybe Tia was right. What she had with Kane was more than she'd thought they'd share. Mutual caring and respect. A deep sexual chemistry and passion. And a willingness to work at the marriage to ensure it really succeeded.

It might not be the ideal marriage, but she was more confident that if she set her mind to it, she could find a way to be truly happy.

River finished packing up the latest batch of nail polish, and then slumped on the couch. She missed Will helping her with this. Of course, she'd known it would just be that one time, but it had been so nice.

Unfortunately, it had ended in disaster. Her heart ached at the thought that she had caused a huge rift between the two friends. She frowned. They'd been more than friends.

She picked up her cell phone and dialed. A moment later, Will picked up.

"Hi, it's River. I just wanted to see how you're doing."

"I'm great." But his voice sounded solemn. "Are things okay between you and Kane?"

She drew in a breath. "They were rocky at first but . . . yeah . . . we seem to be okay. Are you and Kane talking?"

"The only time I've seen him since then is at the staff meeting yesterday and he didn't say a word to me. Other than that, he's kept to himself, and I'm giving him the space he needs. Maybe we'll interact a little more at the board meeting on Monday."

She couldn't imagine how difficult this must be for him.

"Will, I'm sorry I caused this," she said.

"It wasn't your fault. It was my stupid move that caused this mess."

She remembered his *move*. The kiss had been surprising and more welcome than she'd wanted it to be. Maybe because she'd felt so alone with Kane abandoning her so soon after their wedding. Or maybe because it was nice to feel wanted and he was such a nice guy.

But she shouldn't have liked it so much. And she shouldn't want to do it again.

"Is there anything I can do to help?" she asked.

"Just keep trying to make it work. Then maybe with time, he'll forgive me."

"I will. I promise."

"So how goes the nail polish production?"

"I've got about a third of it done. I'm starting on the third color of the collection today."

"You know, you might want to do a batch of each of the remaining colors today."

"But it's more efficient to work on one color at a time."

"Of course. I just thought it might help because of something I overheard Kane saying on the phone, but I'll leave that for Kane to tell you."

Will wouldn't say anything more, and all afternoon she wondered about it. But she followed his advice.

When Kane came home that evening, he found her in the kitchen finishing up dinner preparations. She glanced over her shoulder as she finished breaking up the lettuce for the salad. His hands slid around her waist and he nuzzled her neck.

"My hands are damp," she protested as his lips caressed the side of her neck, sparking delightful sensations down her spine.

"I don't mind." His hands covered her breasts and he caressed her nipples with his thumbs, causing them to pucker.

She leaned back against him, enjoying his attention, her insides heating with need.

He turned her in his arms and kissed her, then nuzzled her cheek.

"A little water won't hurt my suit," he murmured.

She realized that although her arms were around his waist, she'd been holding her hands away from his body, not wanting to ruin his expensive wool suit.

"Are you sure?"

He chuckled and pressed one of her hands firmly on his fine, hard-muscled ass.

"If it does, I'll buy a new one."

She squeezed, loving the feel of his hard, curved buttocks in her hands. He arched his pelvis forward and she could feel his growing erection pushing into her. Her vagina ached with need.

"How long until dinner?" he asked, sparks blazing in his eyes.

"Not too long." She smiled and nuzzled his neck. "But it can stay in the oven a little longer."

The oven timer went off.

He laughed. "Dinner first, then we'll continue this."

She carried the casserole into the dining room. When she returned, he'd finished tossing the salad. They sat down to dinner together.

"Sorry, I mostly know how to cook casseroles."

"I don't mind. But we can hire a cook, if you'd like. I used to have someone come in some days, but mostly I ate out."

"No, I can learn to make other things, too."

"Maybe we could take a cooking class together. I like the idea of spending time together with you in the kitchen, and that seems like a nice thing for two newlyweds to do."

Newlyweds, she thought. She and Kane were anything but normal newlyweds. But then she'd never been one to live life content with being normal.

"I'd like that," she said.

"I was talking to Francoise from Rapture today," he said.

River's gaze shot from her plate to Kane. "Is everything okay?"

"Yes, of course. She has a great opportunity for you. If you can give her a hundred of each color of your collection by this weekend, she'll feature it at the grand opening of a brand-new store in L.A. at the end of the month. There will be a lot of celebrities at the event and it'll give you some great exposure."

Excitement surged through her. The three hundred bottles she'd made before the Kickstarter campaign gave her sixty of each, and with what she'd made today, she was pretty close.

"Oh, my God, that's wonderful."

"I know it's late notice. Can you manage it?"

"Yes, I actually have almost everything I need ready now. And I can finish the rest tomorrow." She smiled. "Thanks to Will."

Immediately, she wished she hadn't uttered those last three words as Kane's expression turned stone cold.

"You talked to Will?" His gaze bored through her. "Did he come over here?"

The insinuation was clear.

"No. I phoned him at the office." She bit her lip. "I just wanted to know how he was doing. You two are so close and—"

"*Were* so close."

"Kane, I know that . . ." Oh, no, she shouldn't bring this up now. That she knew the two men had been lovers.

"You know what?"

She sighed. "I know you really want to keep your friendship with Will and . . ."

"It's not that simple." He glowered at her as he stood up, and then stormed across the room toward the elevator. "I have a meeting. I'll be out late."

Chapter Eighteen

River was still awake when Kane returned—lying quietly in the dark bedroom. When he climbed in beside her, she could smell the alcohol. Within moments, he was sound asleep.

She, however, was restless. In the morning, she got up before him and made breakfast.

When he appeared in the kitchen, freshly shaved and dressed in a nice suit, he poured himself a cup of coffee.

"It smells good," he said nonchalantly. "You can cook more than a casserole after all."

"Eggs and bacon aren't exactly gourmet food, but I know you enjoy them."

She served him a plate with eggs over easy, the way she knew he liked them, and four strips of bacon. She'd even made biscuits. She set the basket on the table and sat down across from him.

"Kane, about yesterday, when I talked to Will . . ."

He frowned. "Let's just enjoy our breakfast, okay?"

"Okay, I promise. But please, don't blame him."

His gaze hardened. "I don't want to talk about it."

His tone brooked no argument, so she turned her attention to her meal, frowning as she picked up her fork.

But she couldn't let it go. Adrenaline surged through her as she focused on her plate, her jaw clenched.

"Maybe you don't want to talk about it, but that's what married couples do." She used her knife to saw through the bacon on her plate. "He's your friend, and he has been for years. I don't want to see that end." She pushed the tattered remains of one bacon strip aside and started on the next. "Don't you get that I care about you and whether you're happy? And I know that having Will as a friend makes you happy."

Then her eyes widened as she realized what she'd admitted. She put down her knife and fork and raised her gaze to his.

He smiled at her, his indigo eyes glowing with warmth.

"I appreciate that," he said.

Then he reached across the table and took her hand. As his big fingers enveloped hers, her heart swelled.

"In fact, I love that you care so much." His velvety voice was filled with sincerity. "So just allow me the time I need to deal with it in my own way, okay?"

She found herself nodding.

He squeezed her hand, his smile broadening. How about this? It's Friday, so once we arrange to send off your nail polish, let's go away for the weekend. Maybe somewhere warm. We could take a long weekend. Just you and me. No one else to distract us."

"But Will said . . . I mean, I understood you have a board meeting on Monday."

Kane frowned at the mention of Will's name, but nodded. "Yes, of course."

"And I probably won't be able to get everything finished until this evening, and then I have to arrange shipping, so we wouldn't be able to leave until late."

His eyebrow arched. "Don't you want to go away with me?"

She reached across the table and took his hand. "Of course I do. I'm just saying I don't think it will work to go somewhere far. Maybe we could just spend the weekend here."

"I have a better idea. Let's go to the house. It has more space and a large backyard with a heated pool. And it's away from everything."

Everything being Will.

"I can't imagine needing more space than here," she said, smiling, "but it will be nice to have a change of scene."

"Good, we can head over as soon as you're done this evening." He finished his last bite of food, and then stood up. He leaned in and kissed her, then disappeared through the doorway.

River finished her own breakfast, then cleared away the dishes and got right to work. In fact, she got into a groove and finished off the last hundred bottles of polish much faster than she thought she would. Of course, the idea of having Kane all to herself for an entire weekend was a great incentive.

She finished packing up the advance shipment for Rapture and arranged with the doorman to have a courier pick up the polishes. Then she decided she'd make good use of the credit card and contact numbers Kane had given her.

Kane got a late-afternoon text from River. He had intended to surprise her and show up at home early, then help her get her polish done and packed up so they could start their weekend sooner rather than later. Unfortunately, a meeting had come up and that plan had gone by the wayside.

He pulled out his phone.

Finished early. Meet me at the house around six?

He tapped in, *Afraid it'll be closer to seven.*

Okay.

At seven-ten, he pulled into the driveway and stepped out of the car. He grabbed the bouquet of roses from the backseat and the bag of Chinese food he'd picked up, along with the cheesecake for dessert. He knew blueberry was her favorite.

He opened the door and stepped inside. A wonderful aroma filled the house. He walked into the living room. The table was set with fine china, crystal stemware, and candles. He walked into the kitchen to see everything in pristine condition. He noticed the oven light on, the temperature on low. But no sign of River.

He placed the food he'd brought in the fridge, then filled a glass vase with water and set the roses inside.

"Hi."

He turned around at the soft, seductive tone of her voice. She stood in the doorway wearing a white satin robe that draped over her body in a way that showed every curve. A *short* robe that exposed her long, shapely legs. She wore white stockings with a thick band of lace at the top—they were the type that would stay up without garters—and high-heeled satin shoes with lace, sequins, and pearls. He recognized them as the shoes she'd worn at their wedding.

And the robe . . .

His groin tightened as he remembered what he'd bought to be covered by that robe.

She hadn't worn his gift on their wedding night, and he'd assumed he would never see it on her. The fact that she'd brought it here . . . that she'd chosen to wear it for him . . .

She stepped forward and turned around, slowly. "Do you like it?"

"I liked it in the store. On you, I *love* it."

He opened his arms and she stepped into them. His lips found hers and the feel of her mouth against his, her soft breasts pressed tight against his chest, sent his head spinning.

He breathed in the soft vanilla scent of her hair, intoxicated by her. Oh, God, he still couldn't believe she was actually married to him. And with her wearing this outfit . . . Somehow it made him feel like she really wanted to be his wife.

His hands glided down her back, then over her round ass. He squeezed, pulling her tighter to his swelling cock. The robe was short enough that his fingertips contacted bare skin. Smooth and soft.

Oh, God, another second of this and he'd rip open the satin robe and feast on her rather than the romantic dinner she'd arranged. He tore himself away and aimed her toward the stove, his hands gliding over her delightful ass one more time, and then he patted it.

"You put dinner out and I'll go change."

"Yes, sir," she said, a seductive smile on her lips.

His cock twitched. God, he couldn't believe how sexy it was when she called him sir.

He strode to the bedroom and shed his suit, pulled on satin pajama bottoms and a matching robe, then walked back into the dining room.

"You learned to cook quickly," he said as he sat down, eyeing the gourmet meal laid out in front of him.

There was a chateaubriand surrounded by truffles and small roasted potatoes, béarnaise sauce, glazed beans with almonds, and a basket of fresh buns.

"I used your credit card and had the meal delivered."

"It's your credit card, sweetheart. To use however you like. Not just for me." He took her hand. "You're my wife."

"Of course."

But he could tell she still hadn't fully accepted that,

which made his heart ache. He wanted her to be his. Completely.

That's why he'd ended it with Will. He loved being with him, but what he felt for River . . .

For a long time, he'd thought it was just an obsession. A mix of his sexual desire for her and a dollop of guilt, which made him want to make up to her for what had happened in college. But when he'd seen her again after all these years . . . as he spent time with her . . . he'd quickly come to realize that what he felt for her was love. Deep and consuming.

That's why he'd changed their business arrangement into a marriage contract. So he'd have time to convince her how much he loved her. And hope that she'd grow to love him, too.

He wanted River as his wife. The two of them a normal, happy couple. It was the way things should be.

Seeing Will kissing her the other day had shaken him badly. He'd thought Will would be by his side, steadfast, helping him with the transition. Helping River, too. But not like that. God, he felt so betrayed.

His gaze fell on River again. So sweet and sexy. So different from him, but drawing him like the moon draws the tides, her immutable allure addictive.

If only she would fall in love with him so they could become a real, happily married couple. Then everything would be perfect.

From the way things were going, this weekend would be a good start.

After dinner, she stood up and cleared away the dishes. He sat and watched the sway of her sexy ass as she walked to the kitchen, enjoying being the cared-for husband. After she took the last dishes away, he walked to the living room and opened the champagne chilling on ice on the coffee table. He sat down and filled the two flutes sitting beside the bucket.

She walked into the room, her body swaying softly, her long legs made even sexier with those shoes. Her long, dark hair cascaded over her white satin-clad shoulders in gleaming waves.

"You look absolutely beautiful tonight," he said, unable to drag his gaze from her.

She smiled. Her fingers tangled in the sash and it loosened, then the robe sagged from her shoulders. His breath caught as the silk drifted lower, parting in front. She let the robe fall away and the sight of her in the white satin corset, her full breasts cupped in white lace, made his heart palpitate.

She was stunning.

His gaze drifted lower, to the small triangle of lace covering her pussy. His cock swelled at the thought that she might be as turned on as he was right now, which would mean she was damp beneath the thin fabric.

Just the thought that she wanted him made his cock twitch.

"Thank you for your lovely gift. Since I didn't wear it on our wedding night, I wanted to wear it for you tonight."

She turned around slowly. The sight of her bare, beautifully round and firm ass made his cock swell another inch.

He stood up and walked toward her, driven by a burning need to touch her. He glided his hands down her sides, loving the sensation of the silk beneath his fingertips. Then the feel of her satiny skin as he cupped her behind. He pulled her against his hard cock, feeling it twitch boldly between their bodies.

Chapter Nineteen

The look in Kane's eyes as he gazed at her took River's breath away.

"You are so beautiful," he said again.

She beamed, loving his adoration. She knew it was the white satin corset that had him so hot and bothered—any woman would look like a sex goddess in this outfit—but she reveled in the joy of being the object of his devoted attention.

She glided her hand down his chest, then over his . . . Oh, God, his cock was so full and hard she was surprised it didn't burst.

She nuzzled the base of his neck, listening to the rumbling moan in his throat as she stroked him. She slid her hands back up and parted his robe, then kissed his collarbone. He untied the sash as she kissed down his chest. She lapped over one bead-like nipple, then teased it with the tip of her tongue. His fingers glided through her hair, and when she started to suck on his small bud, he pulled her tightly to him, murmuring soft sounds of encouragement.

She kissed across his chest and licked the other nipple, then suckled it softly.

"Fuck, baby, I love that."

She glided her finger down his stomach, and hooked it under the elastic of his pants.

"More than when I pay attention to other places?"

He chuckled. "I love it when you pay attention to any part of me, but yes . . . I do have a favorite place."

She pulled the elastic forward and gazed down at the big cock inside. She grasped it with one hand, barely able to get her fingers around it, and then tucked the fabric underneath, exposing his considerable length. She leaned down and kissed the head, the moist tip hot under her lips. She licked him, tasting the salty pre-come.

She knelt, pulling his pants down his thighs and to the floor, then she grasped his big cock with both hands and stroked. His skin glided over the steel column beneath and she longed for that thick shaft to be inside her.

She gazed up at him. "Do you want to take control?" she asked. "Tell me what to do while I call you sir?" She'd seen how his eyes lit up when she called him that. Just like they did now.

"Yes, I do." He stroked her hair. "But not now. Right now I like you being the loving wife. Pleasing me because you want to."

Her breath caught. It was true. She was his loving wife.

She wanted nothing more than to please him. And be loved by him.

But sadly, she could have the first, but . . . not the second.

She tucked one hand under his balls and caressed gently as she stroked his cock.

He wanted her and she wanted him. That would be enough.

"Oh, God, sweetheart." The guttural sound of his words told her he was close already.

She stroked faster. He moaned and his balls tightened in her hand. She knew he was going to come any second now, so she took his cockhead in her mouth. He erupted immediately, the hot liquid squirting deep into her throat. She swallowed the salty seed, taking it all.

When he was finished, she drew back and smiled up at him.

He growled and pulled her into his arms. He took her mouth firmly, his tongue darting inside, and then swirling deeply. She was gasping for air when he released her.

"Now it's my turn."

He backed her across the room, and pressed her down into the big armchair. He knelt in front of her, a predatory smile on his face.

His gaze fell to her breast. He tucked a finger under one of the lace cups and pulled it forward, then tucked it under her breast. Then the other one. His hot gaze made her nipples pucker, the aureoles pebbling.

When his mouth covered her, his tongue swirling over

her hard nub, a moan escaped her lips. He suckled softly and she glided her fingers through his hair, holding him to her. Her whole body trembled with need. She loved having him this close . . . touching her . . . loving her body . . . bringing her pleasure. Another sweep of his tongue then a light nip made her gasp. Then he suckled again. He shifted to her other nipple, leaving the first a glistening tower of dusky rose flesh.

As he suckled, she felt his fingertips graze her inner thigh. Her knees were on either side of him, leaving her open to him. His hand brushed over the crotch of her panties, which was glazed with her dampness.

He kissed from her breast to her neck, and then murmured, "You want me." The whole time, his fingers stroked her lightly, driving her wild.

She held him tightly against her. "Of course I want you."

At the sincere, almost desperate tone of her words, he gazed at her, his indigo eyes searching.

Then he smiled and kissed downward, over the satin of the corset, to her panties. His appreciative gaze locked on them as he tucked his finger under the scrap of fabric and pulled it aside. He smiled, his eyes gleaming.

"Your pussy is so . . . pretty." His finger glided over her soft flesh.

She stopped herself from arching, trembling with the effort, wanting to savor the joy of him looking at her with such avid desire. He smiled and stripped off the panties, then dipped his head down. The moment his mouth came in contact with her, she moaned softly. His tongue teased her flesh, stroking the length of her damp folds. Then he burrowed in, his tongue pushing inside her.

God, this was so intimate . . . so intensely personal. His mouth exploring her most intimate of places. It moved her, and made her wonder how he could do it if he didn't love her. How he could make her feel so special and needed.

But it was just sex. He would do this with any woman who attracted him. And she'd done it with other men. Not many, and every time it had been lacking, at least compared to how she felt with Kane.

Oh, but Lord, with Kane it moved her to her very soul.

His thumb opened her flesh and his tongue brushed over her bundle of nerves, teasing it gently. She arched to him, soaking in the attention, her body opening and blossoming with joy. He nuzzled and teased. Electricity skated along her nerve endings, pleasure coiling in her belly. His fingers dipped into her opening . . . first one . . . then two. They stroked her passage as he suckled on her clit. A craving built inside her . . . for something just beyond reach. A release she needed so badly . . . intensified by every stroke of his finger, every movement of his mouth.

She sensed that he held back. Extending this aching pleasure, wanting to push her higher.

"Oh, please, Kane. I'm so close." She wanted to reach the summit, and ride the exhilaration down the other side, a wild and heady flight of joy.

The feel of his rumbling laughter against her flesh kicked it up a notch. He licked her clit, his tongue working magic, his fingers moving inside her. Her nerve endings prickled to attention and her heart pounded faster. Her fingers curled around his strong shoulders, tightening as the pleasure built within her.

"God! Oh, yes."

It burst within her, like a flame igniting. Intense and overwhelming. Intimate and freeing. Her moan filled the room, growing louder as her body vibrated up the scale of bliss, then exploded into sheer ecstasy.

She collapsed back on the chair, gasping for air.

He smiled at her, then drew her into his arms and held her close. She felt so . . . cherished. His arms around her, so warm and protective. Loving.

"You are so special," he murmured, his breath sending wisps of hair fluttering across her temple. He scooped her up and carried her to the bedroom. He set her down on the bed and stood up.

"Now how do we get this lovely garment off you?" he asked, his gaze lingering over her exposed breasts, the lace still tucked beneath.

"Hooks. Down the back," she said as she reached around and started to release them.

"I'll do it." He sat beside her and flicked open each of the many hooks much faster than she would have managed.

When he reached the bottom, he drew it from her body and tossed it aside. Now all she wore were the stockings and shoes.

He drew her to her feet and his heated gaze traveled her body, making her nearly melt into a puddle on the floor.

"I think you should meet me at the door every evening just like this." His hand glided down her side, sending tingles flashing across her skin.

"You wouldn't get bored?" she asked, her voice breathless.

He glanced down her body and grinned. "You can wear different color shoes and stockings. Maybe sometimes a garter belt."

"What about something like this?" she asked as she reluctantly stepped away from him and opened the top dresser drawer.

She pulled out the long, white gloves from the wedding and pulled them on. He watched her pull the long satin column up her arm, a smile curling his lips.

When she finished pulling up the second, he took her hand and drew her into a deep kiss. Then he stepped back.

"Turn around," he said. "Let me look at you."

She turned in a circle, slowly, her hands on her swaying hips.

The sight of River, her totally naked body framed by the long white gloves and the sheer white stockings, set his heart pounding. God, she was sexy. His cock twitched at the need to be buried deep inside her.

He held out his hand and she rested her satin-clad one against his palm. He closed his fingers around it and drew her close, then pressed her hand against his aching cock. She smiled and wrapped both hands around him, then stroked. The feel of the satin was different. Sexy and new.

She squeezed and stroked faster. He covered her hands and drew them away from his too-close-to-bursting erection, then flattened them on his chest. She stroked over his flesh, the smooth fabric a delight. She glided over his nipples, teased them a little, and then slid over his shoulders. He pulled her against him, her tight, hard nipples pushing into his chest. He slid his hand over her hip and down her thigh, and then lifted her knee, opening her to him. He stroked over her soft folds, dipping into the dampness.

God, he couldn't stand it a moment longer. He grasped his cock and stroked her moist flesh with the tip, then nudged against her opening. But she was so slick he glided in with no resistance, buried halfway inside her before he knew it. At her soft whimper, he pushed in the rest of the way.

Then he simply held her close, her gazing up at him, his cock buried deep inside her. That moment . . . where both of them knew deep in their souls that they each belonged to the other . . . completely and forever . . . moved him.

And in her eyes he saw it. Love. Deep and intense.

And he felt it. His heart pounding with the overwhelming joy that she truly loved him.

He drew in a deep breath, then lifted her other leg. She wrapped them around him as he carried her to the dresser and perched her on the edge.

He tipped up her head, his fingertips resting lightly on the underside of her jaw, and gazed deep into her sparkling green eyes.

He loved her, and he knew his gaze told her that, but he wouldn't say it. He didn't want anything to ruin this moment and saying that, if she wasn't ready to hear it . . .

"I'm going to make love to you now. I'm going to make you come so hard, you won't ever want to leave me."

"I don't want to leave you. Ever."

He smiled. Their gazes remained locked as he drew back and drove forward again. Her eyes widened as he filled her completely. The feel of her all around him took his breath away. He drew back and thrust again. He could feel her quivering in his arms. He kissed her, his lips lingering as he glided in her depths. Out and in.

She clung to his shoulders, arching forward with each of his deep strokes. His cock ached with the need to release and he knew he was so close. But he wanted her right with him.

He stroked her clit and she moaned. He thrust faster, his need coiling tighter.

"Oh, Kane." His name on her lips quivered through him, setting his blood on fire.

He nuzzled her neck. "Come for me, baby. I need you to come so bad."

Quivers rippled through her body and she arched, sucking in air, her legs tightening around him.

"Oh, yes. I feel it." Her words were thin and reedy.

He thrust faster. Deeper.

She cried out in ecstasy as her pussy clenched around him like a soft, tight fist, pulsing. He groaned at the exquisite sensation, his groin burning. Then it happened. A fire deep in his belly, flooding outward. A blaze of heat streaming through his cock. Erupting into her body.

He grunted as he pumped into her, feeling her orgasm humming through him, along with his own. It was magic. Pure ecstatic bliss.

Their pleasure spiraled and flared, taking his breath away, and then quivered to a soft glow.

He sucked in air, holding her tight against him.

Then she giggled. A joyous, heady sound. He gazed down at her, a smile on his face.

"We just had the most memorable sex of my life and you think it's funny?" he teased.

She shook her head and he realized tears streamed from her eyes.

"No. I'm just . . ." She giggled again. "Ridiculously happy."

River set the cutlery on the table. Kane would be home in a few minutes and she had dinner all ready for him. She returned to the kitchen and checked the stew in the pot, a smile crossing her face. She never thought in a million years she'd be playing the role of housewife. Especially to Kane Winters.

Her smile faded as she remembered it was just a role, but these past couple of days, ever since their weekend together, she could almost swear . . .

"Honey, I'm home."

She laughed and hurried to the living room. He said that every evening now. She was surprised he didn't suggest she meet him at the door with a martini.

His teasing suggestion that she meet him in just long gloves and stockings burned through her. Maybe on Friday she'd surprise him and do just that.

As she stepped into the living room, she saw that he'd set his briefcase in the entryway and was walking toward her. He took her in his arms and kissed her. Thoroughly and lovingly. She melted against him, breathless at being in his strong arms.

"Smells wonderful." His smile lit up his eyes.

"I made stew."

"I wasn't talking about dinner," he murmured in her ear.

She stroked his whisker-roughened cheek, longing to drag him off to bed right now. But he'd been making every effort to let her know their relationship was not just about sex and she didn't want to do anything to throw off the fragile balance they'd found.

He followed her into the kitchen and helped her carry things to the dining room. She was still amazed that he was quite happy with the very simple meals she prepared when she knew he was used to gourmet meals. But he understood that's all she knew how to prepare, and that she would be uncomfortable with someone coming in to cook for them. It was heartwarming that he was willing to adapt to make her feel comfortable.

"I was thinking it would be nice to have a party this weekend at the house," he said as he scooped stew into his bowl.

"A party this weekend? But that's not much time to prepare."

"It's no problem. I made all the arrangements today. It won't be a big party. Just sixty people or so. My event planner has it all in hand." He smiled. "I'm looking forward to the opportunity to show off my new wife to my friends."

She shivered. His friends. People she would not be comfortable around.

She speared her fork into a cube of beef. "Why this weekend? Wouldn't it be easier to wait another week or so?"

He smiled. "I want to have it this weekend because I found out today that Francoise, the owner of Rapture, will be in town. I want you to meet her, and she'll be happy to be part of our celebration."

"Celebration?" She gazed at him questioningly.

He smiled and took her hand. "Well, we did just get married."

River sorted through her drawers of nail polish and found the four she was looking for. She grabbed the other supplies she needed and carried them into the kitchen. She lined up the bottles of metallic shimmers on the table next to the little paper cup she'd filled with filtered water earlier and left out to come to room temperature.

She drew in a deep breath, trying to relax. Even though she didn't have to do any of the party planning or preparation, she was still stressed out. She was going to meet Kane's friends. Probably some of the same friends who'd known them in college. Who would remember her as the weird girl whom some of Kane's buddies had bet him to sleep with.

She cringed. Kane had bought her an elegant black dress to wear to the party. Lovely, but much more conservative than she would ordinarily choose. Except for the plunging neckline. It was daring in that way, but she would prefer a flash of color. She would love to do a colorful manicure to grab people's attention . . . but she knew Kane wouldn't want her to do that.

But she wanted to do something special, so she'd pulled out her basic black polish along with silver, gold, and copper metallics. She placed tape around her fingernails on her left hand to protect her skin from the water marble mani she was about to do, then she unscrewed the caps and lifted the black over the water and let one drop fall onto the surface of the water. It spread out in a circle, and she placed a drop of gold in the center of the black circle and watched it spread out. She continued with all the colors, repeating until she had a series of rings in a bull's-eye. She used a sharp toothpick to drag through the polish, first in one direction and then in the opposite direction until she'd formed rows of chevrons across the surface of the water.

Once she had the pattern just the way she wanted it,

she dipped two of her nails into the water. When she pulled them out, she admired the result. Little shimmery metallic and black Vs adorned her nails. She pulled off the tape on those two fingers, and started dropping more polish on the surface of the water.

Kane walked into the kitchen and poured himself an orange juice then walked to the table and watched her form the pattern on the water's surface with the toothpick. He didn't say anything as she dipped her thumb into the water, and then drew it out.

"That looks like a lot of work."

"Not really." She gazed up at him anxiously. "Don't you like it?"

"It's very creative. Are you wearing that to the party?"

Her stomach clenched. "Don't you think it's appropriate?"

"I'm no fashion expert, but I would have thought you'd do something simple and elegant for the party. Maybe something more neutral."

Her back stiffened. "That's not really my style." Feeling defiant, she added, "In fact, I was thinking of putting a purple streak in my hair. Like the kind of thing I used to do in college. Remember?"

Chapter Twenty

River didn't know why she was goading him, but then she realized it was probably because of her nerves. She was coiled up so tight at the idea of this party and being paraded in front of all of Kane's friends that she felt like she'd burst at any second.

"I do remember. But I don't think it's a good idea. Wouldn't it be better if you just try to fit in?" he asked in a persuasive tone.

Her stomach tightened and she had to focus on not clenching her jaw. She hated the fact that he didn't just accept who she was. That he wanted to change her.

He might find her stimulating and sexy in bed, but in life he wanted her to be the model wife who dressed and acted the way he expected.

Then as quickly as her anger had flared, it dissipated.

Why was she fighting him on this? It was only one night, and it was important to him. She had gone into this arrangement of being his wife with her eyes wide open.

He really didn't ask a lot of her, so she shouldn't begrudge him this. And being married meant compromise.

She just wished he could love her for who she was.

She nodded. "You're right. No purple hair."

He squeezed her shoulder. "That's great. I know you're going to look stunning in your dress."

"Thank you," she said flatly, continuing to pay attention to her mani. She'd already decided she'd change it to something more neutral, but she'd finish it now, and then strip it off tomorrow.

"Are you going to be long? I'm heading to bed."

"I'm afraid I'll be up for another hour or so." She didn't look up at him, continuing to drop polish onto the water.

"Okay. Feel free to wake me when you come to bed."

"Why are you sleeping in here?"

River blinked at the soft rays of the dawn sunlight in her face and stared groggily at the door of the guest bedroom.

A very unhappy-looking Kane walked toward her.

She sat up, holding her head. It ached.

He stood by the bed, watching her. Waiting for an answer.

Was he mad?

She squeezed her head, wishing the pounding would stop. "I got to bed really late. I didn't want to disturb you."

"I told you it was okay to wake me."

She tipped up her head and locked gazes with him, feeling a little defiant.

"I didn't *want* to wake you."

She had been annoyed with him. Feeling that she didn't meet his standards as a good wife.

"I didn't mean to come across as demanding last night," he said. "It's just that you're meeting my friends and business associates and I have a better idea of what's appropriate."

"I get it. You don't want them raising their eyebrows and laughing at you because of your choice of a wife. I'm supposed to make you look good, not make you a laughingstock."

He sat down beside her, the bed compressing under his weight.

"I don't give a shit what they think," he said softly. Then he stroked her cheek. "It's you I was thinking of. Yes, some of them might raise an eyebrow at a purple streak in your hair. And I'm afraid that might steal your confidence. I just thought that it would be easier all around if you just try to fit in."

She shook her head. "Don't you get it, Kane? I *don't* fit in. I'm not like you and I'm not like your friends. I really don't know why you ever wanted to marry me."

His jaw twitched and she could just imagine he was regretting his decision about this whole marriage.

She shook her head in resignation. "I'm sorry. I've already agreed not to dye my hair, so why don't we just let it go."

He sighed. "Okay, I agree to drop it . . . on one condition."

Her eyebrow arched. "And what is that?"

Suddenly, he scooped her into his arms. She wrapped her arms around his neck as he carried her down the hall and laid her on the master bed.

"That you agree to sleep in my bed. Every night." He leaned in and stroked her hair, his indigo eyes filled with warmth. "I really don't give a damn about you waking me up. I just want you in my arms."

Then he lay down and pulled her close.

She snuggled into his embrace, trying not to think, ignoring the pounding in her head, and just let the sound of his beating heart soothe her. Soon she fell back asleep.

By the time Kane got home that night, River had dinner in the oven. It was a premade lasagna.

She was in the kitchen finishing the salad when she heard him in the entryway. He didn't call out his usual greeting today, so she kept working. She added the salad dressing.

"Hi," he said.

She turned around to see him standing in the doorway. "Hi," she answered, then turned back to the salad and started tossing it.

She heard his footsteps as he crossed the tile floor. Then his hands slid around her waist and he nuzzled her neck. Her foolish body quivered with delight, while she tried to ignore it.

"Are you still mad at me?" His words brushed against her ear.

She shook her head. She wasn't mad. She was . . . sad.

He turned her in his arms and kissed her. Even if she'd been made of stone, she couldn't have resisted. She kissed him back, accepting the loving strokes of his tongue, loving the feel of his hands gliding along her back, his fingers brushing through her hair.

He drew back, a smile on his face. "Let's eat dinner quickly. I want to take you out for a surprise after."

Over dinner, he talked about some of the plans for the party. It was supposed to be a warm Saturday evening, so the event planner had arranged for lights to be set up on the patio and in the garden, which would be very nice.

After dinner, he helped her clear away the dishes, and then led her from the apartment to his car. She was surprised when he stopped in front of an expensive jewelry store and took her inside.

"I called ahead and had someone bring out a selection for you."

"A selection of what?" she asked as they walked to the glass counter with an array of sparkling gems inside.

When the man behind the counter saw them arrive, he opened a cupboard and laid a piece of black velvety cloth on the counter.

"Good evening, Mr. Winters. Mrs. Winters."

He then began to lay out a series of necklaces that sparkled in the light.

"I want you to pick out a nice necklace to wear to the party," Kane said, his hand squeezing hers.

The man began to describe the necklaces he'd laid out.

There was an oval ruby surrounded by diamonds, and a deep turquoise-blue topaz surrounded by pearls. He'd also selected an emerald, a sapphire, an aquamarine, and her favorite, a stunning fire opal, which was a rich blue with flashes of green, pink, red, and orange.

"They're all beautiful," she said, a bit overwhelmed. "I don't know which one to choose."

The truth was, she didn't want him buying her expensive jewelry, and this type of thing wasn't something she'd ordinarily wear.

Kane wrapped his arm around her waist and pulled her close, then kissed her cheek. "I want you to pick whatever you like. I want you to be happy with it. If you want to look at something else, just look around."

She nodded as another necklace in the display case caught her eye. When she gazed at it, her breath caught.

It was colorful and dramatic, with an array of glittering butterflies of different sizes, looking like they were fluttering away en masse. The palette of colors included shades of blue, purple, pink, red, yellow, and orange. Each butterfly was a single color, but the bodies were set with white diamonds, the delicate lines of their wings radiating outward to deepening tones of the same color.

She loved it. It was so *her.*

But she was sure Kane wouldn't approve.

She sighed and shifted her gaze back to the choices laid out on the black velvet cloth.

"I think the opal one," she said.

"You don't sound very enthusiastic. Is that really the one you want?" Kane asked.

Her gaze fell back to the butterflies.

"You want me to wear whatever necklace makes me happy?" she asked.

"Of course."

She pursed her lips. "What I really like is that one." She pointed at the necklace calling out to her.

"Excellent choice," the clerk said as he brought it out and laid it on the black cloth.

River held her breath, waiting for Kane's look of disapproval.

"That is quite stunning," he said.

River glanced at him in surprise. "Really? You're okay with me wearing that to the party?"

He smiled. "Of course. Why wouldn't I be? It fits you so well."

River stood in shock as the clerk packaged up the necklace in a fancy velvet box.

Could it be that all her insecurities about Kane thinking she didn't fit into his world were exactly that . . . her insecurities? Had she been blowing his comments out of proportion?

Early this morning, when he'd carried her back to the master bedroom, he'd said he'd only been looking out for her feelings. Not wanting her to be hurt by others' comments at the party. She had discounted his words, but now realized that his suggestions last night had been because he was trying to protect her. And as much as she'd like to think she didn't need that kind of protection from him, clearly she was overly sensitive to other people's opinions of her, even if she chose to fly in the face of those opinions. With this party, it was important to her to fit in, and Kane obviously sensed that.

Kane took the bag from the clerk, and offered his elbow to River with a smile. She rested her hand on it and returned his smile.

Was it possible this marriage could work out after all?

When they arrived at the house Saturday morning, River was amazed by how beautiful everything looked. The inside was beautifully decorated with flowers and candles, and the backyard looked like a fairyland, with minilights, outdoor candles, and lanterns. The event planner had done an amazing job.

They took their bags upstairs, then went for a swim and enjoyed the sunny afternoon together. Kane had arranged for the caterers, who were preparing the hors d'oeuvres for the party, to prepare a nice dinner for them, which they ate on the patio overlooking the pool.

Unfortunately, by the time they finished dinner and it was time to get ready for the party, River was plagued by another headache.

Kane accompanied her to the bedroom and fetched a painkiller and a glass of water while she sat on the bed. He watched as she took it, and stroked her hair back with a gentle touch.

"You just relax."

She nodded and lay on the bed, waiting for the pain-killers to kick in as Kane took his shower.

"How are you doing?" Kane asked as he walked into the bedroom from the en suite bathroom and closed the door behind him.

"It's a little better, but I'm going to be late getting ready."

"Don't worry about it. You can be fashionably late. Just come down when you feel better."

She watched him slide off his robe, revealing his naked back to her . . . and his round, firm butt. Then he pulled on his boxers. As he dressed, she concentrated on willing the pounding in her head to go away.

She knew it was just that she was stressed. She tended to get headaches when she was under a lot of stress, and with the total change of her life over the past few weeks, it had definitely been building up.

After Kane left the room, she waited another half hour, but when she heard people arriving, she knew she had to get moving. She didn't want to let Kane down.

She got through her shower and by the time she'd finished her makeup, the pain in her head was just a dull ache. She pinned up her hair, and slipped on her dress. She peered at herself in the mirror as she stepped into the tall shoes.

Just one thing missing.

She retrieved the lovely necklace Kane had bought her. She fastened it around her neck and gazed at herself in the mirror. The butterflies were attached to the chain near her

collarbone on either side, and continued down her chest,
the bottom one nestling between her breasts in a provoc-
ative manner. The lovely colors and line of the piece, set
against the low-cut neckline of the black gown was quite
stunning.

She ran her finger over the delicate, glittering butterflies in awe. They were so beautiful. The fact Kane had
bought this for her still touched her.

She smoothed down her dress and took a deep breath,
then opened the bedroom door. The noise from the party
filled the house. Soft music. People laughing and talking.
She held the oak banister as she walked down the stairs.
She couldn't see Kane anywhere.

Her stomach tightened. She didn't like stepping into
this crowd of strangers. She caught sight of Will and
pressed through the crowd to talk to him.

"You look lovely, River," Will said as she approached
him.

"Thank you," she said as she stepped close.

He introduced her to the couple he'd been talking to.
She shook their hands and immediately forgot their names.
She really wasn't good at this.

"Kane said you had a headache. I hope you're feeling
better," Will said.

Her fingers brushed against her temple. "It's not too
bad now."

He slid his arm around her waist and excused them
from the other couple as he led her to a chair in the living
room.

"You sit here and I'll get you a drink," he murmured against her ear, so she could hear him above the sounds of the party.

She nodded her thanks, and found herself sitting in the middle of the party alone.

"Hello," a tall, platinum-blonde woman said as she sat in the chair next to River.

"Hi," River responded. The woman was quite beautiful, in a polished, sophisticated way. Her gold dress glittered with scattered, clear sequins and her nails were done in a deep crimson red with a smattering of gold glitter.

"That's a beautiful necklace," the woman said with a smile.

River's finger stroked over one of the delicate butterflies. "Thank you."

"So do you know Kane well?" the woman asked.

"Yes, we've known each other since college." River knew she should say that she was his new wife, but she didn't feel comfortable taking the lead as hostess. In truth, she found the woman intimidating.

Will appeared in front of her, holding a flute of champagne. "Here's your drink, River."

"Will, sweetheart," the woman said with a dazzling smile. "I would love a glass, too."

"Of course," he said. "I'll be right back."

The woman watched Will's retreating back, her gaze fixed on his ass.

"He is a sexy man. I hope you don't mind me saying so," she said.

"No, of course not," River answered, and realized the woman thought Will was her date.

She leaned in close to River and said conspiratorially, "Have you ever had the pleasure of"—she grinned—"being with both him and Kane together?"

River's eyes widened.

"Oh, I'm sorry. I've shocked you." She patted River's hand. "It's too bad, because I have and I would love to do it again. But if you and Will are . . ."

"No. Will is just a friend."

"Ah, good. Then maybe I can arrange to have the pleasure again."

The woman's gaze locked on something across the room and River glanced around to see Kane on the other side of the dining room, opening the patio door.

"Excuse me. I'm going to go chat with our host."

Still in shock at the woman's revelation, River watched her stand and walk across the room, the glamorous dress hugging her curves seductively. Should she go after her?

Will returned and glanced around. "Where's Francoise?"

"I don't know," River said distractedly, watching the blonde woman go out the patio door. "I haven't met her yet. I'm sure Kane will bring her over to meet me when she arrives."

"River, you've already met her. She's the woman you were talking to." He held up the glass of champagne he held. "This was for her."

Her gaze shot to his. "She's the owner of Rapture?"

"That's right."

River frowned. "And she had a thing with Kane? And you?"

"She told you that?"

River nodded.

Will downed the glass of champagne.

"Does she know that Kane is married now?" she asked. "Because I got the feeling that she doesn't."

Will pursed his lips. "Kane wanted to wait until he saw her in person to tell her. He was going to introduce you tonight."

"Why? Did he think she wouldn't carry my nail polish if she knew?" She narrowed her eyes. "Oh, God, does he think she's still interested in him?" She rested her hand on Will's. "Is he still interested in *her*?"

"Relax, River. He would never cheat on you. I told you that."

She stood up and started to walk. "I'm going to go find him."

Will walked by her side. "I told you, there's nothing to worry about."

She just nodded, determined to find her husband.

Kane breathed in the night air, trying to clear his head. He'd caught sight of Will with his arm around River's waist, accompanying her to the living room. When she'd sat down, he'd whispered something in her ear. The two of them had looked so . . . intimate together.

He'd almost stormed over and demanded that Will take his hands off her, but he knew he was overreacting.

It had just triggered the image of the two of them kissing that time he'd walked in on them and he couldn't get it out of his mind.

He shouldn't be jealous. In his heart, he knew he could trust Will.

He *thought* he could trust Will.

He raked his hand through his hair. Of course he could.

"Hello, darling."

Kane glanced around to see Francoise walking toward him. He stood in a quiet area of the garden, a little secluded from the rest of the patio, so she'd obviously come looking for him.

"You seem to be struggling with some kind of dilemma," she said in her sexy drawl. "Maybe I can take your mind off it?"

She stopped by his side and rested her hand on his arm.

"Francoise. I'm glad you could come. I want to introduce you to—"

"Yes, I know. This talented new nail polish designer. But not yet, darling." She smiled seductively and stroked his arm. "Tell me. What has you looking so stressed?"

"It's nothing."

She moved in closer and ran her hands up his chest, flattening her palms on his shirt. "I've missed you." Her eyes glittered in the moonlight. "I was so hoping that while I'm here, you and I could . . ."

He flattened his hands on hers to draw them away, but she glided them to his shoulder and pulled him into a kiss. Her lips, so soft and persuasive, reminded him of other nights . . . hot, sultry nights of passion.

He drew his mouth from hers. "Francoise, I can't do this."

"I know. Not now. But after the party . . ." She stroked his cheek. "I hope I can stay over." Her lips turned up in a broad smile. "And maybe we can invite Will again."

"I'm sorry. We can't—"

She pressed closer. "Then just you and me." She wrapped her arms around him and pulled him into a passionate kiss.

Her lips, so soft and pliable beneath his, were pure seduction. But he knew he had to pull away.

At a gasp behind him, he freed himself from Francoise's grip and turned in time to see River marching away.

"Oh, shit."

Chapter Twenty-one

River's heart pounded as she strode back to the house. Will followed her, but when she went inside, she headed straight for the stairs and escaped to the bedroom, closing the door behind her.

She sat in a chair by the window, stifling the tears that threatened. Moments later, she heard a knock, but she ignored it.

Then the door opened. Kane stepped inside and closed it behind him.

"River, let me explain."

"That what?" The words came out sharper than she'd intended. And tears burned at her eyes. "That you and the owner of Rapture are lovers. That you haven't told her you're married because you want to continue fucking her. Or maybe she knows and it doesn't matter to either of you."

"That's not fair, River. I would never—"

"Never what? Kiss another woman?"

He strode across the room and pulled her into his arms and kissed her, stealing her breath away. It almost worked. She almost allowed herself to be swept up in his embrace . . . until she caught the scent of the other woman's perfume on him. She flattened her hands on his chest and pressed him away, then pushed past him and strode to the door.

"I'm not staying here with you. I'm going to ask Will to take me back to the penthouse."

But he grasped her arm. "Like hell you are. I need you to listen to me. I didn't tell her I was married because I wanted to do it in person . . . and introduce you. But I saw you with Will's arm around you, got jealous, and . . . well, fuck, I went outside to clear my head and she caught me off guard. But understand this. *She* kissed *me*. I didn't initiate it. And I didn't want it."

He pulled her close. "I only want you." His eyes blazed with intensity as he stared at her. "You're my wife and I will never cheat on you."

She sucked in a shaky breath. She was mesmerized by the intensity of emotion in those vivid indigo eyes of his.

He squeezed her arms. "Tell me you believe me," he insisted.

Her heart ached as she stared at him.

"I believe what I saw with my own eyes." She glared at him. "Don't treat me like a fool. I saw the passion between the two of you, and it takes two to kiss like that."

His jaw twitched as he met her icy stare.

"I'll stay for the rest of the party," she said finally in a flat tone. "I'll meet your friends, be the loving wife by your side. Then I'm leaving."

She sent him a defiant glance, daring him to protest. He simply frowned.

She held out her hand. "Shall we?"

River put on a smile and stayed by Kane's side during the party, doing her best to hide the turmoil inside. When Kane introduced her to Francoise as his wife, the woman was surprised, but totally unruffled, despite having been caught kissing Kane, and having told River she'd had a threesome with him and Will. In fact, the woman continued to be perfectly charming.

Meeting Kane's friends at the party wasn't as difficult as River had feared. They were all friendly and talkative, drawing her out of her shyness.

The party died down after midnight. Earlier, Kane had told her he'd arrange a car to take her back to the penthouse. Once they saw the last of the guests out the door, she turned from the entryway.

"I'll go get my bag," River said.

As she hurried up the stairs, she realized Kane was behind her. He followed her into the bedroom. She collected her toiletries from the bathroom, tossing them in her overnight bag, and then she grabbed her pajamas and quickly tossed them in, too. She would let Kane worry about the rest. She just wanted to leave.

"I wish you wouldn't go."

She compressed her lips and tried to walk past him,

but he tugged her into his arms and kissed her. His tongue teased her lips open and glided inside her mouth.

God, the man knew how to kiss. She wanted to melt into the kiss. To revel in the strength of his arms around her, and the fact that he wanted her so much.

But she couldn't. She stiffened and pulled herself free, then turned away from him and walked out the door.

River walked to the town car awaiting her in the driveway, blinking back the tears that threatened. When the driver opened the door for her, she saw that Will was inside.

"Mind if I get a ride with you?" he asked.

She slid in beside him. "Of course not, but I thought you were staying for the rest of the weekend?"

That had been the plan. Kane had agreed to the three of them having a nice Sunday brunch and spending the day together, hoping to mend the rift between Kane and Will.

He shrugged. "Yeah, but with you leaving, it's clear Kane would rather be alone, so I decided to head back to my apartment tonight, too."

The driver put her bags in the trunk and got in. The car started to move. River sent a last glance at the house, and then stared down at her hands.

"Do you want to talk about it?" Will asked.

She just shook her head. Her stomach was coiled in knots and she didn't want to have to think about it. They arrived at the building and within moments stepped into the elevator. He pressed the button for the penthouse and for the eighteenth floor, where his apartment was. As the door opened at his floor, she realized that as soon as she got to the penthouse, she'd be alone with her thoughts, and she knew they would spiral around her issues with Kane, dragging her deeper into depression.

"Wait," she said as Will stepped forward. "Is that offer to talk still good?"

He turned to her, his keen eyes scanning her face. "Of course."

When the doors started to close, he pressed the button to open them.

"You want to come to my place?"

"No, I think we should go to the penthouse. In case Kane calls."

Not that she'd answer the call, but . . . she wanted to be there if he did.

"Okay." Will released the button, allowing the doors to close, and the elevator continued upward.

When they arrived in the apartment, he made some decaf coffee while she changed into flannel PJs. They sat on the couch together.

"I don't know what happened between you and Kane after he followed you upstairs," Will said, breaking the awkward silence. But since you're here and he's there, I take it things didn't go so well."

"Are you really surprised after I caught him kissing Francoise?"

His eyes narrowed. "That still doesn't make any sense."

"I know. Because as you've already told me, he would never cheat on me. But how sure of that are you, really? I know you want to believe it. Especially since . . ." She hesitated.

"Especially since what?"

"Well, you were involved with him and when he decided to start seeing me, he ended it with you. It's only natural that you want to believe that it's because he'd never cheat rather than . . ." She bit her lip. "Well, the alternative."

"That he's rejecting me?"

"I'm sorry, I don't mean to hurt you."

Will took her hand, and the warmth and comfort of his big hand enveloping hers was unsettling.

"I know how Kane feels about me. We have a close and lasting friendship. It had an intimate aspect for a while, but I always knew that eventually"—he squeezed her hand—"he'd come to his senses and do something about you."

"About me?"

"He never got over you. He let you slip away, convincing himself it was for the best . . . for both of you . . . but I saw him agonize over his feelings. Then over the years he used to tell me about the powerful chemistry between the two of you, but I knew there was more to his feelings than just lust."

"How?" she asked, wanting to believe.

He shook his head. "I could see it in his eyes. The man

loves you. That's why I kept tabs on you, hoping that an opportunity would present itself where I could get the two of you together again."

"*You* told him about my Kickstarter campaign? But if you were involved with him, why would you do that?"

"Because I care about him and I want him to be happy."

She took his hand. "That's very selfless. You're an exceptional friend."

He laughed without humor. "You probably won't think so after I tell you . . ." He drew his hand away and sighed. "I was the reason everything fell apart between you two."

"No, that happened because of the bet."

He shook his head. "I think it was the recording that really did it." He frowned, looking so somber her stomach tightened. "I'm really sorry, River, but I'm the one who helped them get that recording."

She shook her head as all the pain of that day came tumbling back. Her chest compressed, making it hard to breathe.

"How? *Why?*" she demanded.

"I was short of money—I didn't come from a rich family like Kane and most of his friends. I had to work a couple of jobs to put myself through college, but it was still tough to make ends meet. A couple of Kane's friends told me they wanted to play a trick on someone and they'd pay me to develop an app to hack a cell phone to constantly transmit sound to . . ." He sighed. "Well, the details don't matter. I had no idea they'd use it on Kane's phone or that it would hurt either you or him. But that's no excuse. I should have realized that whomever they used it on would probably be hurt." He met her gaze. "I'm really sorry."

She drew in a deep breath.

"Can you ever forgive me?" he asked.

He shouldn't have done it. And it had certainly caused her a lot of pain. But the agony in his eyes, hinting at the deep burden of guilt he'd been shouldering for years, tore at her heart.

And who was she to judge? She understood needing money to follow a dream, and sometimes going down a path that might be better left untraveled.

She knew Will was a good man.

"Of course I forgive you. It was just an unfortunate series of incidents." She took his hand and squeezed. "And I understand doing something to help attain a dream."

Like marrying Kane. But for the wrong reasons.

As much as she wanted to build a successful nail polish company, deep in her heart she knew she had a dream that was far more important to her.

To have a real marriage with Kane. Based on love.

Her heart ached as she realized *that* dream would probably never come true.

Will gazed into her eyes, shaking his head. "I can totally understand why Kane fell for you so hard. If you weren't his wife I'd . . ."

"You'd what?"

He grasped her shoulders, his eyes flashing with need. She was mesmerized as he seemed to battle with himself, but then he pulled her close and his lips found hers. The kiss was gentle and coaxing. His mouth warm and persuasive. She opened to him and allowed herself to be carried away, not letting herself think about where this was going.

His strong arms slid around her and drew her closer. Some sanity caused her to stiffen.

He drew back. "Aw, fuck, what the hell am I doing?" He stood up. "I'm going to go."

She stood and raced after him. "Wait. Please don't."

He twirled around. "River, we almost—"

"*Almost* is the key word. But neither one of us would betray Kane. We've just proven that." She gazed at him, willing him to understand. "If you leave now, things will just become awkward between us. You'll start avoiding me." The thought of losing him as an ally and confidant knotted her stomach. She'd feel even more alone than she did now. "I don't want that to happen. I like to think you're my friend, and I really need a friend right now. Especially one who understands the situation like you do."

He raked his hand through his hair. "What do you want from me, River?"

"Just stay a little longer. We can watch a movie, or just talk. Anything. Just so we can prove to ourselves that what happened doesn't have to be an issue."

Uncertainty flickered across his hazel eyes, but he finally nodded.

"Okay. Let's make it an adventure film," he said.

Kane barely noticed the bright sunshine and happy twitter of the birds as he left the house on Sunday morning. All he could think about was how he'd blown it big time with River. She'd caught him kissing Francoise and, although Francoise had initiated it, he had to admit, at least to himself, that River was right. It would never have happened if there hadn't been a part of him that wanted it to happen.

And why was that?

He sighed as he started the car and pulled out of the driveway.

He hated to admit that it was because he'd needed to feel wanted. Francoise's desire for him might be shallow and lust-based, but at least she wanted him enough to go after him. River would never do that. If she wasn't in this marriage he'd manipulated her into, she would happily continue her life without a second thought about him.

While he'd never been able to stop thinking of her.

He wanted her to want him so badly. And he wanted her to know how much he loved her. But he was afraid she would reject that love. He'd already felt her pulling back since he'd made that stupid comment about her hair.

By the time he parked his car in the underground garage and strode up the stairs to the lobby, suitcase in tow, he'd decided that he would do his best to work past that.

That today, he would talk to her and find out how she really felt about him. Even if she didn't love him, if he admitted his feelings, maybe they could work together to build a happy, loving relationship.

As he rode the elevator up to his apartment, he began to feel better about the situation. He just had to convince River to listen to him.

The elevator doors opened and he pushed off his shoes and strode to the living room. She might still be asleep and—

He stopped cold at the sight of River nestled in Will's arms, her head resting against his chest, the two of them asleep on the couch. Kane's jaw twitched as his gaze fell on Will's hand, resting on her ribs right beneath her breast. As she breathed, her breast brushed against his thumb and finger. As if he'd been cupping it before they'd fallen asleep.

Anger blazed through him.

River started awake, feeling as if someone was watching her.

"What the fuck is going on here?" Kane demanded.

Then she realized the situation. Her gaze darted around to see Kane standing in the middle of the living room, fuming.

Will sat up and she drew away from him.

Damn. They'd fallen asleep during the movie. It had been a stupid idea to start watching one at three in the morning, especially since she'd already been exhausted by the stressful situation at the party.

She sighed. "Kane, nothing happened between Will and me."

"Nothing?"

The memory of the kiss made her hesitate, and that was fatal.

"Fuck!" Kane's hands clenched into fists and he paced the room. "Tell me."

"It's not her fault," Will said. "It was just a kiss, and that was my fault."

Kane stopped, but glared at her. "But just as you pointed out to me last night, a kiss takes two people."

She stood up. "I'm not going to justify the kiss. I'm just going to point out that we both stopped it and will ensure it never happens again. Because we both care about you."

"How very thoughtful of you both."

She walked to him and rested her hand on his arm. "Kane, I'm telling you that I care about you—both of us do—and I want you to be happy. So I won't do anything that would hurt you."

He shook his head, his eyes telling her there was something she didn't understand.

"Look, I've been thinking about it and . . ." She hesitated, aware of Will in the room. But she needed to make this clear to Kane now. "Well, in thinking about what would make you happy . . ."

The harshness in his indigo eyes softened and . . . she could almost see hope there.

"Yes?" he prompted.

"I think that if you want to, you should be with Francoise."

Kane's eyes widened. "*What?*"

"You said this marriage between us is a convenient arrangement more than anything, so you probably shouldn't limit yourself to just being with me. I know that's the traditional way of marriage, but I think you would be happier if you allowed yourself to be unconventional. Embrace what makes you happy."

"So I would sleep with Francoise whenever I wanted to, and I presume other women, too?"

She nodded, though the thought of him with other women twisted her stomach into knots. She just had to be realistic about what this marriage really was.

"And you," he said in a chillingly calm voice, "I presume you would be free to sleep with Will."

Jealousy and anger flickered in his eyes like a blazing flame.

"No, I'm saying that *you* would be free to sleep with Will. Kane, I know the two of you were involved intimately. And I believe you're in love. But I'm saying that whoever you want to sleep with, it's okay with me. I don't want you to be exclusive because you think it's what I need." She squeezed his arm. "I want you to be happy."

·   ·   ·

What would make Kane happy was if River loved him. But he couldn't say that. And clearly she didn't. She was just in this marriage because of the business agreement, and she would be true to what she'd promised. He could tell she even cared for him. But love?

His heart compressed, and cracked around the edges. He couldn't deal with any of this anymore.

He turned and strode to the bedroom. She didn't follow, probably sensing he needed space to think. But he didn't have any more thinking to do. He tossed some things in a suitcase, enough to get him through a week or so, then zipped it up and strode down the hall.

River's gaze locked on the suitcase, then turned to him. "Kane, what's happening?"

"I've decided it's over. There's no point continuing something that's just not working."

He continued walking to the elevator.

"What do you mean?"

"I mean that this his marriage was a bad idea. So I'm ending it."

Chapter Twenty-two

Shock vaulted through River as she watched the elevator doors close.

Kane had actually left her.

She stood there trembling, frozen while she tried to decide whether to race after him or not. To run down the stairs and catch up with him in the parking garage.

But what would she say?

She turned to Will, searching for reassurance in his eyes.

"Do you think he'll change his mind?" she asked, but the doubtful expression on Will's face did not give her hope.

About an hour later, she received an e-mail from Kane. Very businesslike, clarifying that it was just the marriage that he was ending. They were still partners in the business and she was in control of it. He acknowledged that she'd done her best to make the marriage work and it was he who was ending it so conceded the controlling interest of the company to her.

He also generously gave her the penthouse, which he owned, and even put in a provision that he would pay the taxes and other expenses so she could afford to stay there. In fact, she had no doubt he would offer her a generous divorce settlement.

Not that she cared about any of that. What she wanted was Kane.

Everything about the e-mail tore her heart to shreds. He was loving and generous and really cared about her, but he was ending the marriage. Maybe he didn't love her, but she loved him and she just couldn't let him go.

Will had stayed with her to help her through this. He sat beside her on the couch. He had read the e-mail along with her.

She turned to him and crumpled into his arms. He held her tight, comforting her with gentle strokes down her back.

"I just . . . Oh, God, Will, I don't want to lose him."

"Why, River? You have your life back, and your company. Have you considered that this could be the best thing that could happen to you?"

She drew back and stared at him, shaking her head. "*He's* the best thing that ever happened to me. I love him."

A broad smile crossed Will's lips. "Finally. I was beginning to think you'd *never* admit it. So now the question is . . . are you willing to tell him that?"

It had been three days and River still didn't know where Kane was. He'd responded to Will's e-mails about business matters, but ignored everything else. River didn't try e-mailing him, knowing he probably wouldn't respond anyway.

And she wasn't going to tell him she loved him in an e-mail.

Her cell rang and she picked it up from the coffee table.

Oh, please, let it be Kane.

"Hello?"

"I know where he is." It was Will. "Meet me in the lobby."

River raced to the bathroom and washed her face with cool water, hoping her red, puffy eyes wouldn't be too noticeable, and then she headed for the elevator. Will was waiting for her.

He drove her to a posh hotel downtown and pulled into the entrance. As the doorman opened her door, Will handed her a key card.

"He's in room eighteen sixteen. That'll get you in."

Will had told her he'd used his technical skills to track Kane down using the GPS in his phone, and hacked into the hotel's computer to confirm he was registered. She certainly had no doubt that Will would be able to program a key card for her.

"I'll be nearby. If you need me, just text."

She nodded, then went into the hotel and crossed the lobby to the elevators. Within moments, she was standing outside room 1816 staring at the door.

Should she knock or just walk in? She was his wife, so there should be no problem with her just going inside . . . except that he was here because he didn't want to see her.

She sucked in a breath and knocked. Will had confirmed that Kane was in the room now. At least, his phone was.

She waited, but he didn't answer. She knocked again.

Had he glanced out the peephole and decided to ignore her?

Finally, she pushed the key card into the slot and opened the door. She stepped inside the huge suite. Sunlight shone in the large windows, glistening on the glossy wooden furniture. The place was bright and cheery, flower arrangements filling the room with a lovely fragrance.

But she didn't feel cheery. Her stomach quaked as she glanced around, not seeing Kane anywhere.

He must be in the bedroom.

She walked toward the door, which was open, but didn't see him as she approached.

"River?"

She spun around to see Kane, his broad chest naked and water droplets running down his shoulders from his damp hair. All he wore was a towel.

"What are you doing here?"

"I had to find you," she said. "I need to talk to you."

He frowned and walked across the room to the bar, then poured himself a drink from a crystal decanter.

"I came here because I didn't want to talk. As I said, the marriage failed. Let's just leave it at that." He tossed back the drink and walked toward the bedroom.

He closed the door behind him, and her chest tightened, but she hesitated only a second before hurrying to the door. She pushed it open. Her breath caught at the sight of him, totally naked, the damp towel flung over a chair.

"I told you it's over, River. Just accept that and move on."

"But I don't want to move on." She stepped toward him, intensely aware of his nudity. His broad, muscular body. His big cock hanging down. She wanted to strip down and convince him of how much he wanted her. To show him how good they were together.

But that was sex. What she really wanted to tell him was something much deeper and more lasting.

"What do you want, River? An open marriage where we both have sex with other people? Even if you don't take other lovers . . . that isn't what I want. I want a marriage where we're committed to each other. Where we'll do anything to make it work."

"That's what I was trying to do."

Sadness glazed his eyes. "I know, baby. You were doing the best you could in a bad situation. I don't blame you for it not working. It was just never meant to be."

She stepped toward him. "Kane, please. Can we try a little harder?"

He started to shake his head but she grabbed his hand.

"Please, I . . ." She drew in a shaky breath. "I'll do anything. Because . . ." She stared at him, trying to keep the tears from flowing. "I'm in love with you."

At the shocked expression on his face, she rushed ahead. "I know you don't feel the same way, and maybe by telling you I've ruined everything. But I want you to understand that that's why I'll do anything to make this marriage work. And to make you happy. Even stay on the sidelines while you—"

His lips captured her, cutting off her words.

His tongue delved deep, forcing her mouth wide. He invaded her. Claimed her. And she melted against him.

Was he doing this to shut her up, and then he'd scoot her out the door? Or as a kindness so she wouldn't make a fool of herself and beg him to take her back?

His arms tightened around her and she felt his cock swelling between them. She couldn't help herself. She wrapped her hand around it and stroked. He murmured his approval, but didn't stop kissing her. Then she felt herself tipped back on the bed. His tongue still mastered her as his big, naked body covered her.

She'd worn a skirt and she felt his hand glide underneath and find her panties. He stroked over the thin fabric, then his fingers tugged it aside and he teased her intimate flesh. As his fingers stroked her slick folds, then brushed against her opening, she arched to him, already wet with need.

He shifted and pressed his hard cockhead against her, then watching her eyes, pressed forward. Her breath caught at the feel of his thick, hard flesh gliding inside her. Stretching her as only he could do. She moaned into his mouth as he pushed all the way inside, filling her with his considerable length. She squeezed him, feeling the veins on his shaft throbbing inside her.

She gazed up at him, wide-eyed, seeing the intense need in his eyes.

He had her pinned to the bed, his big cock inside her, unmoving. It was as if it had become a part of her. Joining the two of them. Making them one.

He drew back slowly, and glided inside again. Every nerve ending quivered with joy.

"So you say you love me?" He drew back and glided deep again.

She nodded, her breath quivering at the feel of his long, sensuous stroke.

"Say it," he said.

As if sensing her inability to speak with his cock stroking her, he paused, fully inside her.

She drew in a breath, her gaze locked with his.

"I love you." The words came out breathless.

He smiled. Big and broad. Then he drew back again. And forward.

"And that's why you want to stay married to me?"

She nodded. "Whatever we have to do to make it work. Whatever will make you happy."

He drew back and pushed forward again.

She clung to him. "I'll wear whatever clothes you want, whatever hairstyle or nails you want me to so I'll fit into your life."

His eyes grew fierce and he kissed her hard.

"I've never cared about any of that. I'm sorry I ever

made you feel I didn't accept you for exactly who you are. I only made the suggestion I did to try to protect you. But I should have realized that all you really needed was to know that I was behind you." He cupped her head in his hand and gazed deeply into her eyes. "And I am. Always. I love everything about you. You are *perfect*."

Tears quivered in her eyes, aching to burst free.

"Thank you."

Joy surged through her at the love in his eyes as he gazed at her. And the knowledge that he accepted her just as she was.

"So no more talk of me sleeping with other women. Right?"

She nodded, and squeezed his big cock inside her, sending heat humming through her.

"But about Will . . . ?" he said.

"If you want to be with him, I understand. We can make it work."

"What about *you* being with him?" Kane asked. "What if I'm okay with that?"

She stared up at him, confused. Of course, it was hard to think straight with his thick cock stretching her, and every cell of her body screaming for him to start fucking her in earnest.

"What if I want to watch him fuck you?" he continued, pushing deeper into her. "What if I want to fuck him while he fucks you? What if I want us both to fuck you at the same time?"

She squeezed his cock tightly. Exciting swirls of delight danced through her body at the images he evoked.

He nuzzled her neck.

"Would you like that?"

She nodded before the thought actually formed in her head.

To be with both men would be exhilarating.

"But that doesn't change that it's you I love," she said.

He smiled. "I know, baby. I can see it in your eyes."

He thrust into her, filling her with quivering sensations of delight. His lips captured hers and his tongue stroked inside her, then he began to move. His cock drove deep, again and again. She wrapped her legs around him, opening wider to him. He thrust deeper still and she moaned.

"Oh, God, baby, you feel so good around me."

"Oh, yes," she whimpered as his cock filled her again and again. Pleasure swamped her senses and she clung to him as he took her. Body and soul.

Then he groaned, jerking deep. When she felt his seed fill her, she moaned as bliss exploded inside her, sending her flying to heaven. Moaning Kane's name.

Finally, Kane slumped on top of her then rolled her with him, embracing her tightly.

She snuggled against him, listening to his heart beating, loving being in his arms again.

After a few minutes, he drew away. "Stay right here. I'll be back in a minute."

He left the room and she lay there, wondering how

they would proceed now. She didn't really care, as long as she got to keep being his wife. And making love with him like this.

When he returned, still naked, instead of returning to her in bed, he sat on a chair facing her.

"You're still dressed. I think we should fix that."

She stood up and stripped off her clothes, loving that he watched her with such heat in his indigo eyes. When she dropped the last garment to the floor, he signaled her to come to him. She walked toward him, bathing in the glow of his desire.

She knelt on his lap, her legs on either side of his, and settled on his thighs. His arms slid around her.

"Tell me again," he said, watching her.

She smiled. "I love you."

His eyes filled with tenderness.

"And you really haven't figured out that I love you, too?"

Chapter Twenty-three

River tensed, knowing she must have heard him wrong. "What?"

He smiled. "Don't look so shocked. I've always loved you. That's why I bought into your company and tried to start a relationship with you again. When you flatly refused, I couldn't give up, so I found a way to force you to marry me, so I could take the time to convince you."

She shook her head. "You love me?" The whispered words were full of disbelief.

He laughed. "That's right. I love you."

He pulled her into a kiss that left no doubt in her mind that what he said was true. She could feel it. She could see it in his eyes.

Joy surged through her and she tightened her arms around his neck, throwing herself into the kiss with all of her heart and soul.

When their lips finally parted, he smiled. "Have I finally convinced you?"

She laughed and kissed him again.

"Yes." She snuggled against him.

His arms tightened around her. "This seems like the part where I should propose, but we're already married."

She giggled in joy. "Yes, we are." Life couldn't get any better than this.

"And I promise you, I won't underestimate you anymore. You are a creative, free spirit and that's what I love about you. Instead of trying to urge you to fit in, I'm going to work on changing myself."

Happiness blossomed inside her. She felt . . . cherished. And complete.

"And how are you going to do that?" she couldn't help but ask.

"For a start, I'm going to challenge my own limitations of what an acceptable relationship can be."

"What do you mean?"

"I'm saying that there's no reason I can't be involved with someone else, too."

Her heart compressed in pain and her smile faded.

"But I thought you said . . ."

He cupped her face.

"Don't look so dismayed. What I'm suggesting is that—if you're comfortable with it—that we don't just have a casual threesome with Will, but that we bring him into the relationship. But to be clear, I love you and you are my wife. You will always come first. At any time, if you want us to stop, we will. *You* are the most important person in the world to me."

She cupped his face and kissed him, her head still swirling. All she really understood was that he'd said he loved her and would always put her first.

But slowly the idea of having Will join them in the bedroom sank in. She knew Will and Kane cared deeply about each other. And she was attracted to Will.

Will was sweet and understanding and she knew he cared about both of them and wanted their marriage to work.

"Do you really think we can make it work?"

He smiled. "I do. And if you want to try it right now, Will is waiting in the living room."

She quivered at the thought that he was only a few yards away, while she sat here naked on Kane's lap.

"How . . . ?"

He chuckled. "I knew that he wouldn't be far away, so I texted him to come up. He did give you the key card that allowed you to come in here, right?"

She nodded.

"I'm sure he had one, too." He squeezed her. "So what do you think?"

"I'd like to try it, but I—"

"Will, get in here," Kane called out.

Oh, God, she'd been trying to tell him that she didn't want Will just walking in here while she was naked. But in he walked. Then his eyes popped open and he turned his head away.

"Fuck, man, what the hell?"

Kane chuckled. With her sitting on Kane's lap like

this, both of them naked, Will probably thought they were midcoitus.

River clung tight to Kane, trying to hide her nudity as best she could.

"Will, River and I are together again."

"So I can see."

"And . . . we want you to be a part of what we have."

"What the hell are you talking about?"

"Strip off your clothes and we'll show you."

River trembled in Kane's arms and he tightened his embrace.

"River's being a little shy right now, but we've discussed it and it's what we both want."

Will's gaze turned to River, politely focusing on her eyes. "River? Is this what you want, too?"

As she gazed into his hazel eyes . . . seeing the warmth and concern there . . . she nodded.

His face broke into a smile and he started shedding his clothes.

When he was totally naked, he walked toward them. She couldn't help watching his big cock swing back and forth, growing hard as she watched. He stepped behind her and stroked her back, then knelt down and nuzzled her neck. Quivers danced down her spine.

His hands glided up her sides, then Kane eased her back a little and Will's hands cupped her breasts. She couldn't help moaning as his thumbs brushed her nipples.

"I like watching that," Kane said, his voice low and seductive.

He pushed himself forward and stood up, bringing her and Will to a standing position, too. Then he eased her farther back, watching Will caress her breasts.

"I want to watch the two of you," he said and sat back down.

Will continued to stroke her, then one hand glided down her stomach and he cupped her mound. She longed to feel him touch her intimate flesh. His big, masculine fingers slid over her slick folds, and one glided inside her. Then another. He pushed into her several times, stroking her passage. Sending heat writhing through her.

He turned her and his mouth found hers. His tongue glided inside and he seduced her mouth until she was gasping for more.

"Do you want me, sweetheart?" Will asked.

She nodded, lost in the desire and tenderness in his hazel eyes. He swept her up into his arms and carried her to the bed, then set her down on it.

Soon that big cock of his would push inside her. Gliding deep. Bringing her pleasure.

"But I want to see you with Kane," she said. The need to see the two men together, sharing their love, was overwhelming.

Kane chuckled. "Fine." He came and sat beside her on the bed.

Will smiled as he knelt down in front of Kane, and wrapped his hand around Kane's thick erection. As he stroked it, excitement rose inside River. Watching Will's big man-hand gliding up and down her husband's cock.

She couldn't help herself. She sank to the floor and kissed Kane's tip as Will stroked, and then ran her mouth over his cockhead. Will leaned forward and pressed his lips to the other side of the shaft, then slid off and captured her mouth. He broke the kiss, grasping Kane's cock and taking it into his mouth. She sucked in air at the exciting sight.

Will dove deep, taking all of Kane's impressive length inside.

She was so turned on she didn't know what to do, so she reached for Will's cock and wrapped her fingers around it. It twitched in her hand.

"River, you're holding another man's cock in your hand," Kane said.

"Oh, I'm sorry," she said as she released Will.

Kane laughed. "Baby, I find it extremely hot. I want you to stroke him."

She grasped Will again and began to pump his shaft as she watched him suck Kane. In fascination, she watched his lips glide the length of Kane. Up and down. Heat throbbed through her.

After a few more strokes, Kane stopped Will. "That's enough for now. I want to watch you with River."

Kane drew River onto the bed again and Will pressed between her knees, then he brushed her intimate folds with his lips.

"Oh, God."

Will widened her legs and lapped at her folds. Teasing. Suckling the little petals of flesh.

Then he covered her clit. She arched against him.

Kane's arm came around her and she nestled against his side as he stroked her breast, watching Will pleasuring her.

"Do you like what Will's doing, baby?"

She nodded, enjoying the pleasurable sensations humming through her body.

"His cock is big and hard," Kane murmured against her ear. "Do you want it inside you?"

"God, yes."

Will stood up and before he could press her back on the bed, she grasped his cock and brought it to her mouth. She licked him, and then pulled him between her lips, taking him as deep as she could.

She moved forward and back, taking him deep each time, her tongue swirling along his shaft with every stroke.

Will's cock slid free of her mouth as Kane drew her back on the bed until she was lying across it. Will prowled over her and settled his big body on hers. She gasped as she felt his cockhead brush her intimate flesh.

"I'm going to enter you now, River. Is that okay?"

She wrapped her arms around his shoulders, nodding.

He smiled, and pushed forward. His cock wasn't as big as Kane's but it stretched her nonetheless. He continued forward, slowly. Filling her gently.

When he was all the way inside, she lay quietly, listening to their breathing, as she waited. Letting him lead all the way.

He drew back, then glided deep again.

She could feel Kane watching them. The heat of his gaze filled her with even more excitement.

Will started to pump into her in earnest. Filling her.

"Oh, yes," she moaned.

His big cock glided deep again. As Will pumped, she felt Kane stroke her hair back. He was lying beside her, leaning on his elbow. Watching.

Will thrust deep again and pleasure swelled within her.

"I'm going to come soon, sweetheart, but I won't until you do. Are you close?"

She nodded, delight quivering through her. He pumped deep and hard. She squeezed him, feeling herself slipping into the zone. His finger found her clit and he stroked, making her gasp. Bliss shuddered through her and she moaned, clinging to him.

"Oh, Will, you're making me . . ." The orgasm swelled inside her and she wailed in pleasure.

Every cell seemed to explode in unison as he thrust deep, then again. She sailed the wave of pleasure as he erupted inside her, the feel of the liquid heat blasting her straight to heaven.

She must have dozed off, though she didn't know how that was possible, but then she felt male hands on her, stroking her. She awoke murmuring at the pleasure.

"We want to show you what it's like to be with both of us at the same time," Kane said as he rolled onto his back.

Will urged her on top of Kane and she felt Kane's swollen cock against her belly. She pushed herself up and pressed it to her slick opening, then lowered herself onto him, drawing in a breath at the feel of his thickness gliding deep inside. He cupped her bottom and pulled her tightly to him. He caressed her cheeks, squeezing her around him.

Behind her, Will moved in close. She felt his slick cock brush against her puckered opening. He pressed forward, opening her to him. She stretched around his wide cockhead as he slowly eased inside.

"You doing okay, sweetheart?" Will asked.

She nodded, concentrating on relaxing as his big shaft opened her up. It pushed deeper. And deeper still. She found herself moaning at the unexpected and intense pleasure of both big cocks inside her, Will's deeply immersed in her ass.

"Oh, fuck, baby," Kane murmured. "It's so hot knowing we're both inside you."

She gazed up at Kane, his eyes filled with passionate heat. "Yes," she whispered. "Both of you."

He stroked her hair back as Will nuzzled her neck, sending need quivering through her.

"I want you both. I love both of you filling me." Her hoarse, passion-filled words caused sparks to flare in Kane's eyes and he captured her mouth. Will shifted, sending tremors through her.

Then Will started to move. His cock gliding along her passage. Out, then in. Kane pivoted, his cock moving inside her. Will moved slowly at first, filling her again and again. Kane's cock stroked her front passage.

She trembled with the intensity of it all. Two men sandwiching her between them, their big cocks driving into her. Deeper. Harder. Until she moaned nonstop. Riding the wave of building pleasure.

"Come for us, sweetheart," Will murmured against her ear.

"I want to feel you come as I explode inside you," Kane whispered in her other ear.

"Oh, God." Her whole body heated to the boiling point, then rocked on the edge of forever. The two cocks filled her relentlessly and she clung to Kane as she gasped.

"Yes, I'm coming."

Then sheer ecstasy jolted through her and she wailed. Her whole world shattered into a million pieces as an orgasm of epic proportions carried her away to a blissful euphoria.

The two men pounded deep, then both jerked against her. She felt both of them erupt inside her, their cocks pulsing.

"Oh, yes," she murmured.

The orgasm slowly waned and they all collapsed together.

As she lay gasping between these two sensational men—one her husband and the other his lover . . . and now hers—she wondered if life could ever get better than this.

They unwound and collapsed on the bed in a heap, arms and legs tangled, no one seeming to want to move.

"Is this how it will be from now on?" she asked.

"It will be however you want it to be," Kane said.

Will kissed her cheek. "I'll be here whenever you want me. And if I'm in the way, just tell me to go."

She stroked his arm. "I don't see that happening."

Then Kane captured her lips in a loving kiss. "I love that you've brought us all together, my love. I could never have conceived of this type of relationship before. I've never been happier."

She sighed. "Me, too."

Will nodded and snuggled against her, too.

She glanced at the bedside table, and for the first time saw that Kane had a package of her nail polish collection sitting there. Had he brought it because it would remind him of her?

She knew inside there were the three nail polishes—Arousal, Orgasm, and Afterglow—alongside the two top coats—Passion and Love. Across the box was written the word *Romance*. The sexual theme seemed appropriate to her since the start of her nail polish company was based on her marriage, which she had believed was based on lust. But she had hoped for more. Their marriage had passion, but she also brought love, and now that love sparkled brighter than any holographic glitter ever could.

She had found true romance with Kane.

She fell asleep, knowing that her marriage was all she had ever hoped for, and that life would be even better than she could have ever dreamed possible.